www.HarperLin.com

Cold Case and Cupcakes

A Pink Cupcake Mystery Book 4

Harper Lin

This is a work of fiction. Names, characters, organizations,places, events, and incidents are either products of the author's imagination or are used fictitiously.

ISBN-13: 978-1987859447
ISBN-10: 1987859448

Contents

Chapter One

Traffic on Wolf Road was in complete lockdown. Cars were stalled bumper to bumper as drivers stretched their necks to catch a glimpse of what was causing the delay. All they could see were the back ends of the other cars in front of them.

Amelia Harley looked at her watch. Even though the view from the Pink Cupcake food truck was better than that of her neighbor in the sedan, she could only see the long snake of traffic and the flashing lights of squad cars up in the distance.

"An accident," she mumbled. "Someone speeding, or maybe a car broke down."

With the truck in park, she reached into her purse and fumbled around for her phone. She called home and smiled when her son answered the phone.

"House of insanity."

"Adam, are you really answering the phone like that?"

"Hi, Mom. No. Sometimes I answer, 'Harley Estate of Madness.'"

"Great." Amelia chuckled. "So long as people don't think we're crazy."

"Where are you? Meg's threatening to turn cannibal if you don't get home soon." Amelia's daughter, Meg, could be heard in the background, yelling the word *brraains* like a zombie from a horror movie.

"I'm stuck in traffic. There was an accident or some kind of incident on Wolf Road, and everything is backed up for miles." She sighed. "Tell Dan when he gets there that I'm trying to get home."

A bubbly beep went off in Amelia's ear. She lowered the phone and saw the familiar number of Detective Dan Walishovsky, who should have been pulling in her driveway at this very moment.

"Honey, Dan is on the other line. I'll call you right back." With a little more fumbling, she pressed the green telephone image and listened. "Dan?"

"Hi, Amelia." His deep voice on the other end of the line always gave Amelia a slight shiver when he spoke. It was that macho just-the-facts tone that she couldn't resist.

"Hey. I'm so sorry, but I'm stuck in traffic. I'm going to be late, so you and the kids can go ahead and get started. Just make sure they save me some spaghetti, because I'm starving." She spat all the words out in one breath.

"I'm afraid that's my fault." Dan groaned. "We've got a situation at the No-Tell Motel, and the ambulance and black-and-whites have bottlenecked the street."

"My gosh!" She stretched her neck as if she could see something, but the view hadn't changed. "What happened?"

"Without giving out too many details, we've got a dead man here. Looks like a suicide, but..."

Amelia could tell by Dan's voice he was already working the case. Something wasn't right. There was a wet towel or a torn-up newspaper or some other weird oddity that made him think the scene wasn't what it seemed.

"I've got some leftover cupcakes in the truck. Would you like me to drop them off for you and your officers when I get closer? I'm literally down the street."

She rubbed her stomach as she thought of the spaghetti waiting for her at home. Since she baked cupcakes all day every day, that was the last thing on her list to eat. However, if she had a spaghetti-and-red-gravy cupcake in the back of her truck, she'd eat it and not share. Her mind began to toss around the idea as Dan spoke.

"Not this time. It's too much of a risk for contamination. We haven't swept the parking lot yet."

"Okay, well, I know the kids will be disappointed."

"Just the kids?"

Amelia clicked her tongue and rolled her eyes.

"No. I'm disappointed too. But I know how work can be. Do you want to come by when all your paperwork is done?"

"It's going to be a pretty late night. I think I better take a rain check."

"Okay, Detective. Be careful."

Without another word, Dan hung up on his end. It was one of his little quirks that he rarely said good-bye to Amelia when he hung up the phone. Just as he would tuck her hair behind her ears if a few short wisps got out of place.

It wasn't the first time Dan had cancelled due to work. It was one of the hazards of dating a detective on the Gary Police Department. But Amelia had *really* been looking forward to tonight. Adam, Meg, and Dan were all free. The spaghetti was just the glue to bring them together. They were going to eat in front of the television like bad people do and watch one of Meg's all-time favorite movies, *Soylent Green* with Charlton Heston.

"He's dreamy," Meg gushed when she got to pick the movie of the week.

"What?" Adam couldn't keep from making a comment. "He's like a hundred years old, and he's losing his hair."

"Yes, but he's got that something. Mom knows. He's a detective in the movie like Dan is."

Amelia shook her head at her daughter's observation but smiled. The fact she thought Dan was good enough to be compared to the late Charlton Heston was a pretty big accomplishment. No badge of honor bestowed on any uniform could quite match it.

She called home again.

"Mom, are you almost here?" Now it was Meg's turn to whine. "I'm starving."

"Looks like Dan can't come. He's been called to investigate something at the No-Tell Motel."

"Eww." Amelia was sure Meg was wrinkling her nose on the other end of the phone. "I've heard that place has bed bugs, and that's the *good* review."

"You guys go ahead and get started without us. I'm still in traffic, and it doesn't look to be moving, and he doesn't have any idea when he'll be done doing what he needs to do."

"Okay. We'll save you some."

"Thanks." Amelia sighed.

"Mom's spaghetti is people!" Adam yelled in the background. "People!"

"I'll be home as soon as I can."

Meg could be heard laughing at her brother as Amelia ended the call. She slumped behind the wheel and wondered what could be taking so long for the police to get traffic moving again.

To take her mind off being hungry, she tried to plan her day for tomorrow. But the idea of a spaghetti-flavored muffin just wouldn't let her go.

"People don't eat muffins with spaghetti. They eat bread or garlic bread. The time it takes to make bread might be too much," she mused to herself.

She thought that people *did* eat cornbread. That was really more like a muffin. And, a lot of time, they ate it with chili.

"So how could I get the taste of chili in a cornbread muffin without the mess?"

Her stomach grumbled.

"If I baked it inside the corn muffin, just a teaspoon or something. Garnish with a sprinkling of cilantro and a jalapeño on top." She wasn't sure if this was a good idea or not. Her leftover double-chocolate-fudge cupcakes were sounding better and better.

"You'll ruin your appetite," she scolded herself and called for backup. But, instead of backup, she got voicemail.

"You've reached Lila Bergman. Please leave a message." *Beep.*

"I'm stuck in traffic. Where are you when I need you?" Amelia teased her. "What do you think of a corn muffin with a dollop of chili in the middle with cilantro and jalapeño on top? Call me back."

Lila was hired just as Amelia was starting The Pink Cupcake. It was one of the best decisions she'd ever made in business and in her personal life. Lila had quickly become a priceless employee and a trusted friend.

Amelia leaned back in her seat and started to stretch just as her phone chirped and made her jump.

"I'm sorry," Lila snapped into the phone. "I am ignoring my calls, but when I saw your number, I was too late to answer it."

"Why are you ignoring your calls?" Amelia was immediately suspicious. Lila had a few health issues that she was keeping close to the vest, and it was in Amelia's nature to assume the worst right off the bat.

"Because I've got a brother threatening to come to town and I told him I was not taking in strays at the moment."

"I didn't know you had a brother."

"Yeah, we don't really get along. He's weird."

Amelia smirked. "Sort of the pot calling the kettle black, I'd say."

"He's not weird in a good way like you. He's weird in an annoying and aggravating way. I made the mistake of telling him about my visits to the doctor. No children. No spouse. Where will my fortune go?"

"No. You don't really think that's what he's thinking, do you?"

"He wouldn't be Bobby if he didn't. I'll bet he has a coffin all picked out and an urn just for backup."

"Lila, please don't talk like that." Amelia gasped. "You aren't dying."

"No. I'm not. I'm not anywhere near that, but that doesn't stop Bobby's wishful thinking." She snorted. "Remind me to tell you tomorrow about how his wife manages to get placed in the wills of all kinds of people who aren't related to her."

"What?"

"It's true. Her best friend is seventy-nine years old. My sister-in-law is only thirty-six. What kind of thirty-six-year-old woman has a best friend forty-three years older than her? But trust me. When the woman dies, my brother and sister-in-law will be the beneficiaries. It's a very lucrative hobby."

"It sounds kind of sinister."

"Morbid. That's the word I'd use."

"Yikes, can we change the topic? What do you think of my idea?"

"Oh yes, chili muffins? Fantastic idea!"

Talking with Lila managed to kill some time. Finally, traffic slowly began to creep forward.

"I gotta go, Lila. The cars are finally moving. I'll see you tomorrow."

"Are you going to make those chili corn muffins tonight?" Lila murmured.

"You sound like you want me to."

"Well, if you've got nothing better to do. I'd love to sample one. Sounds like a great breakfast muffin for people who crave something savory instead of sweet."

"Good point." Amelia rubbed her growling stomach. "I'll see what I can do."

After they said their good-byes, Amelia tossed her phone back in her purse, put the car in drive, and slowly started to inch her way up as the cars ahead began to move.

As she got closer to the No-Tell Motel, Amelia couldn't help but notice how conflicting the landscaping looked: beautiful blooming red flowers around the sign advertising hourly rates and Jacuzzi suites.

The parking lot and two stories of rooms looked clean enough, but Amelia saw one of Dan's uniformed officers standing outside the motel office with a man who she assumed was the proprietor. He looked how she expected an hourly-motel office manager to look. He wore tan pants that had seen better days and a T-shirt affectionately known as a "wife-beater." Chest hair that matched his forearms bubbled out the top. In his hand, which was more like a paw, he had a stogie. He wore flip-flops because he assumed people wanted to see his feet.

Amelia also saw Dan's car in the parking lot, but the detective was nowhere to be seen.

At long last, she was able to press down on the accelerator and push the needle dangerously close to fifty miles an hour in a forty-mile zone. With a little luck, the lights remained green along the way, and Amelia happily walked in the door, greeted by the delicious smell of spaghetti and the sound of her kids talking together like movie critics. It was wonderful to be home.

After Edward G. Robinson's tearful suicide and Charlton Heston's feeble attempt to save humanity, Amelia strolled into the kitchen and began pulling ingredients out of her cupboard.

"Mom, can I go to Shooshies?"

"What's at Shooshies?" Amelia asked, looking at the expiration date on a bag of cornmeal. "Did you break a wheel on your skateboard?"

"No. Nothing. Just a couple of the guys from school were talking about hanging out there."

Amelia looked up at her son. He was taller than her. Spending all that time in the dark basement he'd converted into his room must have helped him grow, because last time she looked, he was clinging to her thigh with a binky in his mouth.

"Be home before nine. School tomorrow."

He agreed and grabbed his skateboard and left out the front door.

Going back to her cupboard, Amelia found a can of Hormel chili. Meg stood up from the couch and stretched her arms over her head.

"That movie has a sad ending." Amelia looked at her daughter.

"It does. But sometimes life is sad." The provocative thought came out of her fifteen-year-old daughter's mouth in that cute singsongy way she spoke.

"I hope for you that's not very often." Amelia set the can down on the kitchen table and went to the fridge. Fresh cilantro and jalapeños were in the crisper.

"I was just thinking the same thing about you." Meg pulled her long brown hair over her right shoulder.

Amelia turned around and looked at her daughter.

"Me? Why would you be worried about me being sad? Do I look sad?" Amelia clenched her teeth together and pulled her lips back like a snarling dog. Meg laughed.

"No. You look psychotic." She stepped up to the kitchen table and began to trace the wood grain with her finger. "I just think sometimes you might miss the way things used to be, you know, when you and Dad were still together."

Amelia heard the words and turned to look at Meg.

"Do you miss those days?" Amelia was afraid to hear the answer. When she stepped back and looked at her life now compared to where it had been, she couldn't believe it was hers. Her business was doing better than she could have imagined. Her kids were doing well in school. Dan had become an important person in her life. But as she looked at Meg, who was still so innocent but had to face the all too grown-up issue of divorce, she couldn't help but feel she had been selfish.

"Sometimes," Meg mumbled. "But I don't think The Pink Cupcake would have ever existed otherwise. Plus, we probably would have never met Dan, and I really like him."

"You do? What do you like?"

"His stories. He told me once how he chased this drug dealer into an alley when he was still a uniformed cop. The guy waited for him and then jumped out with a knife." Amelia gasped. She hadn't heard this story and wondered why Dan had shared this particular tale with her daughter. "Dan grabbed the guy's hands in his and then head-butted him, knocking him out cold."

Meg watched her daughter's eyes widen and blink as she concluded the harrowing story.

"He also told me one about a snitch that...."

"Okay, okay. I get the idea. You mean you like those stories better than the stories I used to tell you before bed? You always liked the one about the princess and the pea." Amelia grabbed her cutting board. Placing it on the table, she pulled a large knife from her chopping block and began to slice the jalapeños after she had turned the dial to warm the oven. "Of course, I always added a few embellishments to the story."

"Yeah." Meg laughed. "The princess went to sleep on a watermelon, a turnip, a sack of potatoes, and I think you even threw in a wild boar and Emma Jackson, that little brat who used to pull my hair in kindergarten."

"So Dan's stories are better than mine?"

"Well, they are different, that's for sure." Meg looked at her mother with questions in her eyes. "Is that okay?"

"Well, I don't know if I like you knowing about drug dealers and snitches, but..."

"Mom, we watched *The Man with the Golden Arm* with Frank Sinatra two years ago. And I saw the edited version of *Goodfellas*, so I know what a snitch is."

"Good heavens, how much television are you watching?"

"It isn't quantity, Mom. It's quality."

Amelia pursed her brow then shrugged.

"Speaking of quality, did you get your homework done?"

"Did it in study hall."

"So what are you going to do now?"

Meg looked around the kitchen and then to her mother's ingredients spread out on the table.

"I don't know. Need some help?"

Amelia looked up and smiled. "Yes."

She explained her new muffin idea and got an enthusiastic seal of approval from The Pink Cupcake's biggest supporter. After all the prep work and in between gossiping, Amelia and Meg put the ingredients together, adding just a pinch of sharp cheddar. That was Meg's idea. When the timer had gone off and they pulled the new concoction from the oven, the Tex-Mex muffin had been born.

"Lila is going to love this!" Meg boasted, licking her fingers.

"And I love you. Thanks for the help." Amelia kissed her daughter's head.

"Save one for Adam," Meg insisted, which Amelia obliged, putting one away in a special plastic bag separate from the rest she'd take to work tomorrow.

Her children were so good. What she had ever done to deserve the two greatest blessings of her life, Amelia didn't know. But she thanked God for it every day.

Chapter Two

Food Truck Alley, as it was affectionately known in the city of Gary, had become Amelia's home away from home. Over the past several months, her list of friends had grown as much as her business.

Len from Charming Wok, who made incredible egg rolls, knew exactly what Amelia meant when she praised the customers who paid in change.

Henrietta from Heavenly Soul Food treated both Amelia and Lila to a heaping helping of her red beans and rice and, like Amelia, had also put in several calls to the city to get them to manage the grass and trim the trees and shrubs where the trucks were parked.

Connie from That's Amore Pizza collected the leftovers from several of the trucks every Thursday and took them to her church to donate to their soup kitchen.

Then there was Gavin, the Philly Cheese Steak guy and Amelia's neighbor to the left, who encouraged building businesses together by sending his customers to The Pink Cupcake for dessert.

After having lunch with Gavin a couple months ago, Amelia felt a little awkward when he came around.

It was like a high school football star suddenly noticing the bookworm girl in study hall. Why? What was the angle? Amelia knew it was wrong to assume Gavin had an angle, but she couldn't help it. She didn't see herself the way he saw her. Plus, this was her job. She had paid for this space on Food Truck Alley with her own hard-earned cash. She wasn't going to jeopardize it for a pretty face.

Lila, on the other hand, had no problem gossiping with the handsome Philadelphia native. Today was no different. But the news he shared sure was.

"Did you guys hear about the murder yesterday?" He stood outside the order window, leaning casually against the truck while sipping his coffee. Every day after the morning mayhem, but before the lunchtime lunacy, Gavin would stop by.

"Murder?" Lila asked, looking over her shoulder at Amelia, who was busy prepping the area for the next round of cupcakes to keep the lunchtime crowd happy.

"Yeah. At the No-Tell Motel over on Wolf Road."

"Murder?" Amelia looked up. "I thought it was a suicide!"

Both Lila and Gavin looked at Amelia with their eyebrows pinched together in the middle.

"Dan was supposed to come by last night, but he couldn't because he was stuck at the No-Tell Motel." She looked toward Gavin as she spoke. "He said it looked like a suicide. But he did sound unsure."

Amelia stepped closer to the window.

Gavin pulled out the Gary local newspaper. There it was as front-page news: "Prominent Los Angeles reporter found dead in motel. Police suspect foul play."

"They said the guy was in town looking into a cold case from about ten years ago." Gavin scratched his perfectly square jaw. "Some kid was murdered."

Lila gasped. "I remember it. That little boy who was found dead at Rochester Playground? He'd been beaten and strangled and dumped there. That was a heartbreaking story."

Amelia took the paper and began to read the details. David Scranton was the reporter's name. He had a long list of credentials, including bylines in *The New York Times*, *Newsweek*, *Chicago Tribune*, *The Economist*, and a handful of other journals.

"Weird," she mumbled.

"What's weird?" Lila turned.

"That little boy–Dwight was his last name, if I remember right." Amelia looked up at Lila. "He was beaten but died from strangulation. This says David Scranton was strangled, too. But he had cuts on his wrists."

"Yikes," Lila whispered. "That is weird. I wonder what Dan's opinion is."

"Who is Dan?" Gavin asked.

Amelia snapped out of her daze and shook her head.

"Detective Dan Walishovsky. Close friend of mine." She couldn't quite bring herself to say boyfriend. She was in her forties, after all. Man-friend sounded like some kind of prehistoric animal or a creature from a horror movie. She looked at Gavin, who she suspected caught her meaning but didn't seem to be bothered by it. *That* bothered Amelia.

"Well, I've got to get back to work." Gavin smiled up at Lila.

"Don't work too hard, Gavin." She waved and turned her back.

"I promise," he replied. "See you later, Amelia."

Amelia nodded and waved.

"What is the matter with you? Why are you so rude to him?" Lila teased her.

"Was I rude? I don't know, Lila. He's nice and good-looking, but there just isn't that spark."

"Not like there is with Dan?"

Amelia couldn't control the smile that crept over her face.

"Never mind, Amelia. No need to answer. Your red cheeks say everything."

The women continued to prepare for the midday rush even though a blanket of dark clouds started to roll in. It would probably put a dent in the number of patrons visiting Food Truck Alley that afternoon.

Amelia was thankful for that. She was distracted.

She recalled the sad story of the case David Scranton was researching. The details were hazy, but in a nutshell, that little boy was only six and had been strangled and left in the dirt at the playground. Thankfully, he was discovered in the early hours by the city garbagemen long before anyone showed up at the park to play. Many people blamed the mother, but no one was ever caught.

The whole situation reminded her of the panic California residents experienced in the 1980s when Richard Ramirez–The Night Stalker–was on the loose. Girls with long hair cut their hair short because some of his victims had long hair. Two homes he had broken into were beige, so anyone who had a beige or brown or off-white house gave their homes a new face just to deter him from singling them out. People were reporting anything that appeared out of the ordinary, and any stranger driving or walking down the street soon had a squad car or two pulling up behind them and officers stepping out of their cars, hands on their pistols just in case.

The town of Gary had experienced that fear, too. But it was like a desperate whisper, not the scream of the California residents in the '80s. Since only one child had died and there were no other missing children one week, two weeks, a month, three months later, it was decided the mother had something to do with it. The story went from a headline to a tiny paragraph buried on the blotter page with Travis Foggarty being fined for shooting a BB gun at a stop sign and an unseen vandal throwing a rock through a window at the high school.

Nothing ever came of the case. That little boy was buried, and with him went his story. Now, a decade later, a reporter with a long line of credentials had decided to look into it, and he turned up dead, too.

Lila was right. Amelia did want to talk to Dan about the story and see what she could find out. But she knew he wouldn't say too much. He couldn't. It would go against his nature of doing things by the books. But if she collected her own arsenal of facts and asked him what he thought, she might be able to piece something together.

As predicted, a steady downpour of rain that decided it wanted to remain all afternoon hampered the flow of customers. However, even with this setback, The Pink Cupcake managed to end the day over two hundred dollars in the black.

While driving home, she decided to stop at the grocery store to pick up the ingredients she thought would make a good chili for the Tex-Mex muffins.

However, she couldn't get out of her mind the story of the reporter and that little boy from ten years ago.

As she got back in the car and headed home, she let herself mull over the tragedy and why it bothered her.

It was simple: Adam and Meg. They were six and four years old when it happened. Adam had been the same age as that boy. Her children had grown into such beautiful individuals. But that boy's mother would never get to experience that.

It was a pain Amelia didn't want to imagine. She couldn't imagine it, not really, since her children were at home, safe and sound, young adults who were smart enough not to take candy from a stranger or open the door for someone they didn't know. Still, the sad story made her push the accelerator down further on The Pink Cupcake truck just to get home a few minutes faster.

When she walked in the door at 6:30 as she did almost every day, she felt a wave of relief when the first sound she heard was her little angels arguing like an elderly couple.

"I told you to set it over there!" Adam scolded Meg.

"What difference does it make if it's here or there?"

"It makes all the difference in the world. But you are just too much of a simpleton to know that."

"Aren't you a big shot. A simpleton. How long you been waiting to slip that funny word into a conversation?" Meg's sarcasm was a trait she inherited from her mother.

"Hello? Is this the most happy and joyful home of Adam and Meg O'Malley?"

"Hi, Mom," the kids replied in unison.

"What's going on?" she asked while carefully tiptoeing into the kitchen.

"Meg's just screwing everything up," Adam said matter-of-factly as he scooped up his schoolbooks and headed toward his room in the basement.

"He's griping because I set the phone over on the counter instead of on the table, and he wanted to snatch it up in case Amy called. As if I don't know they've got the hots for each other already."

"Okay, okay," Amelia said, setting her purse and a few leftover cupcakes on the table. "That's enough."

She shook her head then walked up to Adam and mussed his hair.

"Did you do your homework?"

"Yeah." He rolled his eyes.

"Did you guys make sandwiches for yourselves? I promise to go to the store and get real groceries this weekend."

"Yes, and Adam ate all the dill pickles, as usual." Meg snitched as she turned and headed upstairs to her room.

"You say that like it's a surprise." Amelia unpacked the grocery bag with ingredients to make chili.

"I really need to get my own apartment." Adam sighed as he headed down into the basement.

"You said it, not me," Amelia teased him as she went about getting her giant soup pot from underneath the counter.

* * *

As the ground beef browned in a pan and the garlic and onions simmered in the bottom of the soup pot, Amelia set up her laptop on the kitchen table and typed in the name *Dwight*, the word *murder*, and the city of *Gary*.

There it was. The same article she had read ten years ago along with the picture of the victim. Preston Dwight. He was six years old, smiling at the camera while holding what looked like a teddy bear in one hand and a little train engine in the other. His hair was going in several directions as if he'd just woken from a nap.

Amelia remembered when Adam would wake up from his naps, his eyes fresh and his hair wild, as if bats had nested in it while he slept. He'd run back to whatever project he'd been working on before he had been forced to lie down, and the adventures would begin. His little hands would push cars and airplanes to their imaginary destinations. Brilliant battles would be fought between plastic army soldiers. The good guys always won. The bad guys always went to jail.

The sad story of Preston Dwight gripped her heart, and she couldn't help the tears that surfaced in her eyes.

"What a shame," she muttered. Swallowing hard, she shook off the hat of mother and slipped into the cap of sleuth.

She scrolled through the rest of the article, noting three valuable bits of information. The mother, Starla-Ann Dwight, the baby's father, Kyle Spoon, and the boyfriend, Timothy Casey. All were considered persons of interest, but no arrests were ever made. She quickly wrote the names down in a notebook.

There was a listing for an S. Dwight. The other two names were not listed, but that didn't mean anything. Lots of people were unlisted. Amelia herself was unlisted.

"Well, it's as good a place to start as any."

Amelia went back to the beef sizzling in the pan, lifted it, and drained off the excess fat. She'd have three dozen Tex-Mex muffins to unleash on her customers tomorrow.

And then a quick trip to the home of Starla-Ann Dwight.

Chapter Three

Brookhaven was a neighborhood in the periphery of downtown Gary. It was like the corner of a yard where the trash cans were kept. There was very little grass. Passersby would mostly see broken glass, filthy newspapers, or plastic bags lying around that had escaped the trash man's compactor. The place was dirty and secluded, and most people avoided it if they could help it.

Amelia looked at the map on her phone, which was attached to the dashboard. If she went up two more blocks, she should see Combs Street, where she needed to take a left. It was marked with several pairs of shoes hanging from the telephone wires.

As she made the turn, she found it difficult to tell which houses were actually being lived in and which ones might be abandoned. Metal bars were on most of the windows. Others were covered with plywood. There was a scattering of homes that displayed their owner's care with flowers and wind socks and colorful flags that read "Welcome" or "God Bless America."

The majority of homes were sad, run-down structures that still held the ghosts of their majesty and beauty, like the architectural details of a round attic window or a brick chimney.

Even if they wanted to be lovely homes again, the effort would be null as long as the owners left hundreds of neon-colored children's toys dumped carelessly around the sparse patches of grass, or worn-out sofas positioned on the front porches as they did now.

A few characters who dared venture from their homes watched Amelia as she slowly drove past. While she'd left the pink truck at home, the sedan she drove was an unfamiliar car to them, so she was on their radar now.

One man in a sleeveless flannel shirt, baggy sweatpants, and no shoes stood on the edge of his porch steps, a cigarette in one hand and a cell phone in the other, studying her with a cold stare.

Amelia could feel herself sweating. Maybe it wasn't such a good idea to come here alone. She had followed her heart, but what if this was dangerous? Nobody even knew she was here.

Finally, she rolled up to the address she had been trying to find and let out a sigh of relief. It was just a plain bungalow. There were black bars on the windows, but Amelia was still able to see curtains being parted then quickly falling back into place.

She climbed out of the car, slinging her purse onto one arm, trying to act as if she were just visiting an old friend, but she felt she looked more like a nervous ten-year-old stepping onto a stage to recite five words for the school Christmas pageant.

Before she could knock on the screen door, the heavy inside door was yanked open, and a scratchy female voice spat, "Can I help you?"

Amelia widened her eyes innocently as she carefully approached the screen door.

Calling it a screen door was really open to interpretation since the screen hung lazily from the corner, easily letting in any winged devils it was designed to keep out. The bottom of the metal frame was bent outward as if it had been kicked.

"Excuse me, ma'am. I'm looking for Starla-Ann Dwight?"

"What for?"

Clearing her throat, Amelia wasn't sure what to say next. What did she want to speak to this woman for? What business was it of hers to ask her about what was probably the most horrific experience of her life?

"I don't know," Amelia confessed. "My name is Amelia Harley. I heard about your son's death being looked into, and I thought I might be able to help. I think I made a mistake," Amelia grumbled. "I'm sorry to have bothered you."

Quickly, she turned and took a step toward her car.

The broken screen door scratched open.

"Hold on," the woman said, leaning out the opened door.

She looked exactly like her voice sounded: a bleached blonde with jet-black roots and deeply wrinkled skin from too many tanning sessions. She looked out the door at Amelia. Her brown eyes were devoid of eyelashes, and her eyebrows had been plucked into near nonexistence. She wore a baggy men's T-shirt and, despite the cooler temperature, spandex shorts that exposed her wrinkly knees. "Did that reporter send you? He said he was going to come by."

Amelia blinked in surprise.

"You mean David Scranton?"

"Yeah, that's the guy. He stopped by here last week and said he was coming back. That he saw a lot of flaws with Preston's investigation."

"No. I'm not with him," Amelia sputtered. "I guess you hadn't heard, but he was found dead in his motel room."

The news barely caused the woman to blink.

"That doesn't surprise me." Licking her lips, she surveyed her estate then held the screen door open wider for Amelia to enter.

"Why not?" Amelia asked.

"Because I know someone who wouldn't want the case to be reopened. Come in."

Amelia gave an awkward grin and stepped into the house. It smelled of many years of cigarette smoke, as did the woman who held the door for her.

"Starla-Ann died about three years ago." The woman walked past Amelia to a worn-out sofa and grabbed a pack of Marlboros and a hot-pink lighter. "I'm her sister, Sandra."

"I'm sorry." Amelia stepped to the sofa and took a seat on the edge. Sandra sat in a swiveling La-Z-Boy, kicked back, and crossed her legs. She shrugged at Amelia's condolences.

"It doesn't matter." She spoke with the cigarette between her lips. "She died the day they found Preston. It just took a little longer."

"Sandra, do you have an opinion on what happened? I know what the newspapers said. I watched the reports on the news. But what do you think?"

"Why are you so interested?" Sandra took a deep drag, and the smoke poured out of her nostrils as if she were a mad bull.

"Because my little boy was the same age as Preston when he died. Because I have a daughter two years younger. Because I think it is terribly unfair, and if nothing else, I wanted someone to know that people do care."

Amelia felt the sting of tears in her eyes. She didn't know where they were coming from and felt foolish sitting there like that in front of a woman who obviously looked rode hard and put away wet, as a workhorse would.

Sandra rolled her eyes.

"It was that no-good SOB Kyle Spoon who did it." Sandra acted as if the name just coming from her mouth were bitter poison on her tongue. "As sure as I'm sitting here, he killed that little boy."

Kyle Spoon was in the newspaper report about the killing. He was Preston's biological father, although he and Starla-Ann had never married.

"But those papers you talk about getting the story from had my sister tried and convicted before the baby's body was even cold." Sandra reached over to a TV tray and grabbed what looked like a beer in one of those keep-it-cool gloves. It could have been a Pepsi, but Amelia kind of doubted it. "Don't get me wrong. Starla-Ann wasn't the sharpest pencil in the box, but she loved Preston. She'd have died a thousand times over if that would bring him back." She took a swig from the can then followed it with a drag on her cigarette. "They said that because of where she came from. Needless to say since the Kennedys moved out, the neighborhood has sort of gone downhill."

Amelia couldn't help but chuckle at Sandra's sarcasm.

"But my sister was just one of those good kids. Not the 'good kids' you read about now." She made air quotes as she continued, "Who get shot in drug deals or drive-bys and their mothers weep about them being 'good kids' who supposedly were always laughing, always ready to help. Bull."

Sandra laughed at her own comment.

"No. Starla-Ann was a real good kid. As soon as she found out she was pregnant, she got on them baby vitamins and made me go outside to smoke. I still feel a little funny doing it in the house now." She clicked her tongue.

"How old was Starla-Ann when she had Preston?"

"She was eighteen. Old enough. Kyle Spoon was twenty-two." She pinched her lips. Amelia couldn't tell if Sandra was going to cry or scream. She did neither.

"Starla-Ann couldn't wait to have that baby. And when he arrived, screaming and wailing, Starla-Ann laughed out loud. *He sounds like me, Sandra*, she said in the delivery room. I remember her smiling so proud." Shaking her head, Sandra finally let a small grin through. "She did everything she could for that baby. When he died, she did, too. Every day he was gone, she died a little bit more, till finally there wasn't nothing left."

"Who took care of him?" Amelia asked.

"Are you kidding? Starla-Ann took care of that baby. She worked at the Hardee's over on Plaza Drive. Like a storm, she marched in there and told them she needed a job to support her baby and could work every day but no later than five. Wouldn't you know, she got that job. Was assistant manager within two years and hoping to start managing the place just before..."

Amelia felt the pain Sandra was holding back.

"They wanted to make her out to be average white trash. Like she was sitting around collecting welfare. You know why they thought that? Because of Kyle Spoon, that's why."

Her demeanor changed instantly when she spoke about Preston's father.

"There wasn't a scam or dirty deal that man wasn't involved in. In and out of prison, and not even for a crime that might give a man bragging rights. He couldn't even do that right."

"How did they meet?" Amelia noticed pictures of Starla-Ann and Preston in a prominent place just above the television.

"He was pretty well known around town. If he looked at a girl like Starla-Ann, well... it was all over."

Amelia's eyebrows shot up.

"Starla-Ann was smitten." Sandra took another drag. "That was the only thing Kyle had going for him. He was good looking. Could have done a lot with that face and body, but too stupid to figure that out. Instead he neglected his brain and thought with his you-know-what."

"Was it just a one-time thing?"

"Oh, no. Unfortunately, they thought they'd play house and make a go of things. Starla-Ann would have been better off to cut him loose as soon as she realized he wasn't planning on getting a job. But she thought he was watching Preston while she worked."

"Was Preston with Kyle when they first realized he was missing?"

Sandra took another long swig while nodding her head.

"By this time, Preston was six, and Kyle had been in and out of the house, getting thrown out for coming home drunk then talking his way back in. He was the only man Preston called Daddy. But he was gone most of the time. He usually found his way back when Starla-Ann had a new man."

"Did she date a lot?"

"Not really. I think she was always hoping for Kyle to fix himself up and get serious. I think she dated some of these guys just to get Kyle jealous and coming around."

Sandra went on to describe a few of her sister's boyfriends. They were all the same. Blue-collar guys with muscles and tattoos but no real future. Except for Timothy Casey.

"Tim was a good guy. He was a plumber's apprentice. As soon as he completed the hours he needed, he had plans to go into business for himself. Toilets always need to flush, right? He's got his own business now, from what I've heard."

"Well, that sounds pretty stable. What happened with him?"

"Preston disappeared. Those couple of hours he was gone felt like a lifetime, not just for Starla-Ann, but for the rest of us, too. Kyle was at the house. Starla came home to no baby and went on a terror like you never saw. Once the police arrived and took their statement, putting out the Amber Alert and all that, Tim showed up, and all hell broke loose. Like two male gorillas facing off for the prize of leading the pack. Kyle and Tim got into a fist fight in the front lawn. Starla-Ann was screaming and crying, neighbors were in the yards watching, laughing. Things didn't calm down until both men were cuffed and in the backs of separate squad cars."

"Did they question Kyle then when they brought him to the station?"

"I guess. They cuffed those two idiots in a couple of chairs. I'm sure they sat there like two boys in a pissing contest giving each other dirty looks but neither one making a move. They were asked what all the hubbub was about, and then the cops turned them loose. Meanwhile, my sister is going crazy with grief and worry, and Preston, that beautiful little boy, he was still out there."

"I don't understand. How did Kyle explain Preston not being in the house?"

"Kyle said he fell asleep," Sandra spat. "The boy used to go outside sometimes looking for his mom right before she would get home from work." Sandra smiled. "My sister had a ritual with him that when she got home from work she'd grab him and kiss all over his face like she hadn't seen him in weeks instead of just a few hours. He loved it. You should have heard him giggle."

Sandra explained how the police said that was the most logical explanation. Preston wandered outside. A stranger picked him up then dropped him in the park when it was dark.

"But I know it was Kyle. He hid that boy's body then dumped it as soon as he got a chance." Sandra smoked her cigarette then stomped out the smoldering end in an ashtray that was home to half a dozen other butts.

"Why do you think the police didn't make any arrests?"

"Do you really not know the answer to that? Did you have on blinders when you drove here? We don't count. Let the community decide who did it, and maybe they'll chase the riffraff from town and save them the paperwork."

Amelia sighed. What could she say? Even though she no longer lived in the upscale neighborhood she had before the divorce, she was still living in a pleasant area where she wasn't afraid of her neighbors and the grass was green and the streets were paved.

"I'm not some bleeding heart, Miss Harley. I'm not looking for something for nothing. I'm just tired of there being a big hole where my sister used to be. Where my nephew used to be. And I'm sick of knowing that SOB is still walking the streets."

"Do you know where he lives?"

"Yeah." Sandra tapped another cigarette from the pack and placed it in her mouth. "He spends just about every waking minute at the Sovereign Tap."

"That's over on Halstead, right?"

Sandra nodded as she lit the cigarette.

"But don't be surprised if you don't get anything from him. His brain is so pickled now I don't even think he remembers. A guilty conscience will do that to a man, you know–prevent him from facing what he's done."

Amelia nodded then stood from her seat.

"Thank you for talking to me, Sandra." Sticking her hand out, Amelia watched as Sandra stood from her La-Z-Boy and wiped her hand on her T-shirt before shaking.

"If you're going to talk to that piece of filth, tell him I hope his liver is good and rotten and causing him a great deal of pain."

Amelia nodded.

"If I learn anything, if I hear anything, I'll let you know, Sandra. I promise."

Sandra nodded, but the expression on her face told Amelia she was used to hearing that. Without another word, she turned and walked toward the door, letting herself out.

Chapter Four

Once in her car, she let out a deep breath and sank back into the seat, letting her muscles relax for the first time since she arrived.

She drove past the same bare-armed hillbilly on the way out of Brookhaven.

Once on the main road, Amelia hit the gas and headed toward Halstead and the Sovereign Tap. The clock on her dashboard said it was almost seven o'clock. Meg called, and she accepted it, happy to hear her voice.

"Hi, Mom. Can Katherine stay for supper?"

"If she wants. What are you making?"

"I thought you were bringing home burritos or something."

"Yeah, I was going to do that, but I'm running behind on my errands. Can you get with your brother and order some kind of delivery? There is money in the cookie jar."

"Can we get Wing Ho Chinese?"

"Only if your brother agrees. I don't want a bunch of drama over what to get for dinner."

"Okay. When do you think you'll be home?" Amelia could hear Meg telling Katherine they were getting Chinese food just as she pulled up to the blazing sign that read Sovereign Tap.

The letters on the marquee in the window informed customers that they cashed checks and a six-pack of Miller Light was $7.99.

"I'll be home as soon as I can. Love you."

"Love you too, Mom."

Amelia hung up and climbed out of the car.

The Sovereign Tap was a liquor store in the front and a bar in the back. She walked through the blinding fluorescent lighting, past the gray-looking cashier on his cell phone, and approached the black doorway with the word B-A-R over the top in neon red.

She wished she had worn just jeans and a T-shirt. She felt terribly overdressed in her black pants and gray sweater. Even her earrings made her feel like Princess Grace stepping onto an oil rig.

Blinking madly, she let her eyes adjust to the dark and her ears adjust to the noise from the jukebox.

This place smelled the same as Sandra's house but with a hint of stale beer added to the mix. The lighting was exceptionally low, making it look a thousand times more elegant than it was in reality. It also helped the patrons look less haggard.

Sitting dangerously close in the very back booth by the jukebox was a couple talking quietly into each other's faces. There were a couple of glasses in front of them. The woman sipped a beer, licking her lips afterward. Her companion was balding, and his pinky ring winked in Amelia's direction.

At the bar, two fellows stared up at a television that had some kind of ballgame on. Once in a while, they made remarks to the bartender and each other about what they were watching.

Then there was a large man sitting by himself with a bottle of beer and an empty shot glass in front of him. Amelia took a deep breath, trying not to cringe at the smell of smoke, and walked over to where he was and sat down one barstool over.

The bartender gave Amelia a double take, making her reach up protectively to smooth the nape of her neck.

"What can I get you?"

Amelia quickly realized she had to order. Of course. How could she forget such a ritual to the bar-going experience?

"Can I just get a Coke for starters?"

Without a word or another look, the bartender nodded and grabbed a thick tumbler, loading it with ice. He took the hose that provided the drink to fill the glass and dropped a straw in the concoction.

When he was done with Amelia's order, he went back to the other side of the bar with the guys to watch the game.

Amelia took a sip. It tasted like any other Coke, to her relief.

How would she know if Kyle Spoon showed up? She didn't know what the guy looked like except that he was big and good-looking, and that wasn't even a guarantee. Ten years and the grief of a child's death could greatly age a person.

She could ask the bartender, but she had seen enough movies to know that that probably wasn't a good idea. People who hung out in bars like this usually didn't want people coming around asking about them. Bartenders knew that.

She looked in her purse, briefly considering the idea of a bribe. What was the going rate of bribes these days? Was twenty dollars enough? Fifty? She didn't have either and was pretty sure her six dollars and forty-two cents would get her shown the door. At least that was enough to pay for her Coke.

A few minutes later, the bartender made the rounds, coming back to ask the man next to Amelia if he wanted another.

The man nodded without saying a word, took the bottleneck, and tossed the last bit of it down his throat. The bartender pulled out a bottle of something that looked brown and poured it in the shot glass. With another swift move, he slid open the cooler, pulled out another beer, popped the top, and placed it in front of the man.

"Get hers, too."

The man jerked his head in Amelia's direction.

"Thanks." Amelia smiled.

The man at the bar chuckled, his broad shoulders shaking slightly.

"I'm Amelia." She dove in headfirst. There was no way she was going to get any information just sitting there.

"Kyle," the man grumbled, smiling pleasantly and reaching out his hand to shake.

Amelia's heart jumped. Could her luck be that good today?

Leaning forward, she took his hand and looked at his face in the dim light. He was handsome, but she wished she had a little more information to go on.

"Nice to meet you."

He nodded, and Amelia could tell he was trying to think of something to say but was obviously out of practice as much as Amelia was. She didn't have time to play coy either if she was going to get information.

"You wouldn't happen to be Kyle Spoon, would you?" Amelia held her eyes to his even as his square jaw set tightly.

"Amelia. Do I know you?"

"No. You don't."

"What can I do for you?" He took the shot glass, tossed it back, then grabbed the beer and took a sip.

When he looked at her full on, she realized he was handsome. But the past few years hadn't been kind. Amelia wasn't captivated by his spell, but she could tell why a girl like Starla-Ann might fall for him.

He looked like Superman with dark hair, huge broad shoulders, and big hands that could be protective or menacing depending on his mood. He was in jeans and a flannel shirt with work boots that had to be size fourteens if not bigger.

She saw the telltale sign of a beer gut beneath that flannel. His nails were chewed to the quick. His teeth were straight but stained yellow from tobacco, and he hadn't shaved.

"I wanted to ask you about Preston."

A shadow fell over him, his face freezing into stone.

He signaled to the bartender then tapped the shot glass in front of him. Like a trained monkey, the bartender came over, poured another three fingers' worth in the tiny glass, and then left again.

"Would you mind if I asked you a couple of questions?" Amelia scooted over to the empty barstool that was between them, closing the gap. It was a risky move. She had no idea what Kyle's temperament was like. Aside from yelling loudly, Sandra never said he struck Starla-Ann or Preston. But there was a first time for everything.

After tossing back the shot and chasing it with a long swig of beer again, Kyle hunched over the bar.

"How did you know where to find me?"

Swallowing hard, Amelia cleared her throat.

"Sandra Dwight told me."

He laughed bitterly.

"I'll bet she told you it was all my fault, too. I bet she told you I killed my own son. Didn't she? Did she tell you that I went out with her before Starla?"

Amelia froze.

"I'll take that as a no." Kyle reached into the breast pocket for his cigarettes. He banged a fresh pack against the heel of his palm while he smiled at Amelia. He pulled off the cellophane and silver top and offered a smoke to Amelia, who shook her head no. "Are you a cop?"

"No. I'm not."

He leaned in so close to Amelia that she could feel his breath against her cheek.

"Then what are you doing in a place like this, nosing around in business that is none of yours?"

She didn't move or flinch but turned to face him squarely.

"When a child is murdered in the town I live in and no one is ever caught, it becomes my business." She didn't blink and let out a deep breath as if she were waiting for him to finally say something worth listening to.

Leaning back, Kyle lit his cigarette and, as Sandra had half a dozen times, took a long drag off it. For a second, the tip of his nose and his chin glowed an eerie red from the burning tobacco then faded away.

"I see. Aren't *you* the tough one." He hissed. "Are you here to tell me I should kill myself too? Is that it? Like Sandra told me to do? Like half this town told me to do? Have you got some sixth sense that has told you I'm the man who did it? That I'm guilty?"

Amelia shook her head. This big brute was starting to get excited, and who knew what he'd be capable of doing in a fit of rage.

"No." Amelia's voice was soft but firm. She couldn't show any of the fear that was running through her veins like a swarm of fire ants. "I only want to know your story, your side of things."

"Okay. I had tossed back a six-pack and got drunk. I fell asleep, and the next thing I know, Starla-Ann is beating on my chest and head to wake me up, screaming that the kid was gone." He took another gulp of beer. The cigarette he lit smoldered in the ashtray in front of him. "I thought she had seen her sister leaving and was pissed about that."

"What?"

"Oh, Sandra forgot to tell you that, too? Funny, she forgot to tell the cops about it, too. Yeah. She knew I was back with Starla. She also knew Starla wasn't home yet and that there was a good chance I had beer, so she stopped by. She wanted to act like we never broke up, if you catch my meaning." He winked at Amelia. "But I wasn't that drunk. Don't get me wrong. Sandra was a good-looking woman when she fixed herself up. But I don't crap where I eat."

"Why didn't you tell the police she was there? That could have made a big difference in the investigation."

Kyle tapped the long gray ash from the end of the cigarette.

"No, it wouldn't have." He sneered. "It would have just caused me a lot of explaining."

He looked at the row of bottles in front of him. Amelia sat patiently waiting. Kyle Spoon was a textbook case of alcoholism and much too far gone for her to try and help. All she could do was listen.

"Sandra was good in bed. No doubt. But Starla-Ann, well, she was different. Preston looked just like her, too. He looked so much like her that there was almost no trace of me anywhere except in his feet. The little guy had clodhoppers just like his old man." He looked down at his huge work boots.

"So you didn't tell the police that Sandra was there. You kept a secret for her. Yet she still doesn't like you? I don't get it. Why would that be?"

Kyle shrugged.

"Come on. You're a woman." He snickered.

"So Starla-Ann never knew her own sister was trying to steal her man?" Amelia sipped her pop as Kyle shook his head no.

"Where were you when Preston was found?"

"I was sleeping off the beers I had that night. I didn't think it was anything serious. I was sure they'd find him and that he'd be okay and everything would have worked out fine and gone back to normal."

He drank down the last of his beer. Looking at Amelia's nearly full glass of soda, he chuckled.

"Would you like another one, or is that one going right to your head?"

Amelia grinned but shook her head no. "Sandra said there was a fight, too, that night. Is that true?"

The smirk left Kyle's face, and he looked toward the door of the tavern.

"Boy, Sandra sure felt chatty. Did she tell you that fella just came waltzing in the house like he lived there?" He clenched his fists. "Did she tell you it was my house Starla was living in?"

"That made you mad?"

"Look, I doubt you'd know what it feels like to see the father of your children with someone else." His eyes roamed up and down Amelia's body, making it obvious he approved of what he saw. "But when it's at your own home, I feel I got the right to take a swing at the man."

Amelia couldn't bring herself to tell him she knew exactly how it felt. She didn't want to have anything in common with this guy who drank his dinner every night and graded his women on how they were in bed. But still, the first time she saw her ex-husband, John, with his new girlfriend, Jennifer, she did want to slap them both.

"Plus, I didn't like the look of the guy. One of those know-it-all types." Judging from Kyle's behavior, Amelia thought it was just a simple case of the green-eyed monster. If the new boyfriend was working and wanted his own plumbing business someday, while Kyle was only testing the capabilities of his liver, there was no doubt there would be a clash of horns.

"Did Starla-Ann call her new boyfriend to come over?"

"She must have. I certainly didn't do it."

"Sandra didn't do it?"

Kyle sat there for a moment and stared at Amelia. It was obvious he had never thought of that. Then he snapped out of it and shrugged.

Amelia looked sadly at Kyle. It occurred to her that he had talked about everyone involved in what happened that night except Preston.

"Well, Kyle, I appreciate your talking with me."

"Leaving so soon?" He looked at his watch. "I thought in a little while we could swap recipes and discuss women we hate then binge on some chocolate."

There was a tinny sound in his voice as Kyle spoke. He knew what he was. His looks were fading. He had no real job and probably got paid under the table so he could continue to collect some kind of social security or disability or whatever program he could swindle from. This was as good as it was going to get. He didn't even have his son to carry on his name. It was more sad than anything else.

As Amelia slipped off the bar stool, she stuck out her hand to shake.

Kyle looked at it and then up at her eyes.

"You know..." He smiled a smile Amelia knew he had practiced on dozens of women over his lifetime. "If you'd like to stick around and see what happens, no strings attached, I'd be good with that."

Pulling her hand away quickly, Amelia tilted her head to the left and pursed her brow.

"Good night, Kyle."

He laughed loudly as Amelia left. She was happy to be back into the bright fluorescent light of the liquor store, and the fresh air outside made her lungs feel free to expand and fill up.

She climbed into her car and had just strapped her seat belt on when Kyle came hurrying out of the building. He saw her in the car and came up to the driver's-side window.

Rolling it down just an inch, Amelia smiled awkwardly at him.

"I wanted you to know that I didn't kill my son."

"I didn't say you did, Kyle."

"No. I know. Thanks for that. But." He stuck his hands in his pockets for a second then withdrew them again. "I never did anything with my life. Preston was my only accomplishment. Preston was the only thing I was ever proud of."

Without another word, he strolled back into the Sovereign Tap.

Chapter Five

After Amelia had gotten back home and spent almost a solid half hour under a hot shower, scrubbing off the stale smoke smell, she put on some comfy sweats and sat at the kitchen table.

Making up the menu for The Pink Cupcake tomorrow gave her some relief from the horror story that was the murder of Preston Dwight. She couldn't help but wonder why the police didn't look into this whole situation more.

The father, who was known to be in and out of trouble with the law, had a little boy who turned up dead, and no real questions were asked? It didn't make any sense. How could Sandra get away with not mentioning she was at the house the same night the boy disappeared?

Amelia tried to focus her eyes on the two suspects. The only one who said anything about David Scranton was Sandra. He had contacted her and told her why he was in town? Could she have been more involved than she'd let on?

Just then the doorbell rang, making Amelia jump out of her skin.

"I'll get it!" Meg yelled and came stomping down the stairs like Coxey's Army. "Hey, Dan," Amelia heard her cheerfully say. "Come on in."

"Thanks, kid. Mom home?"

Amelia stood up, running her hand through her hair, and walked toward the front door.

"This is a surprise," she said to Dan.

He was carrying a big white take-out bag. He followed her into the kitchen and set the bag on the table. The rich smell of hamburgers and French fries hit Amelia's nose and made her stomach grumble.

"Oh gosh. Are those Moody's burgers?"

"Only the best for you."

"Well, you're a keeper." She turned to grab a plate, when Dan took her by the arm and squeezed. Both looked in Meg's direction, but she had already disappeared back upstairs.

Amelia smiled as Dan leaned down for a kiss. He smelled good, wearing the spicy cologne she liked so much. Not a trace of cigarette smell.

"Let's eat," he finally said after holding Amelia close to him for several seconds.

After Amelia poured some water into a couple of glasses, they sat down across from one another and began to eat.

"So how's the case coming along?" she asked between bites.

Dan dabbed a drop of ketchup off her chin with a napkin.

"This is a strange one," he said. "Without making you lose your appetite, I'll keep the details to a minimum."

"I don't mind details." Amelia leaned forward, eager to hear what Dan had to say.

"I knew there was a reason I liked you," he teased her. "This Scranton guy had been at the motel for several days prior to his murder. There is some evidence that he was not alone."

"Like someone else working on the story with him?"

"Not quite. More like someone else keeping him company."

Amelia's eyes widened as she nodded.

"We found some physical evidence that was out of place for a guy there alone."

"Like what?"

"Well, there were candles in the bathroom where the body was found. There was also an empty condom wrapper on the floor next to the bed."

"But how did he die? I thought the papers said he was strangled."

"That was how he died. However, whoever did that to him wanted it to look like either a suicide attempt or some kind of kinky escapade gone wrong."

"I'm confused."

"You aren't the only one." Dan took another huge bite of his juicy burger before continuing his description of the murder scene. "Scranton was strangled to death by what seemed like a unique-looking cord that had a zigzag pattern down the middle of it. But whoever strangled him also slit his wrists in an attempt to make it look like he killed himself. He was placed in the bathtub with most of his clothes still on, and there was no suicide note."

"I'm exhausted just hearing that." Amelia took a drink of water. "That is a lot of work to go through, and what for? What did Scranton know that he had to be killed for?"

"Call me crazy, but I don't think he was really here to investigate the cold case of Preston Dwight. I think it was a ruse to do something else. But someone *thought* he was here to do that and didn't want him digging up any old bones."

"Why do you say that?"

"Because the cord used to strangle David Scranton had the same pattern as the cord used to kill Preston Dwight."

That tiny fact sent shivers up Amelia's spine.

"Are you going to visit the suspects in the original murder of that little boy?" Amelia swallowed hard. "Because I already met his aunt. She said she spoke with Dan Scranton. It seems that Preston's mother, Starla-Ann, died not long after Preston did."

"Those people are from Brookhaven, Amelia. That isn't a safe place for a lady to drive in alone."

"It was broad daylight, and I knew where I was going."

"But I didn't know where you were going." Dan let out a long sigh. "What in the world possessed you to go there by yourself? Can I just ask that one dumb question?"

He leaned forward and looked Amelia in the eye.

"Dan, Preston was six when he died. Adam was six that same year. I can't imagine what that mother went through. To have the case go cold. I guess I just wanted to tell her that she wasn't all by herself. That people cared. I don't know, that sounds stupid. But it's true. I know if it were me, I'd appreciate a kind gesture like that. Especially if I came from what everyone knew was the wrong side of the tracks."

Amelia let out a deep breath.

"The next time you decide to go to Brookhaven or some other ghetto by yourself, let me know ahead of time. At least I can have a couple of squads nearby in case you need help."

“I guess I should tell you that I spoke with Preston’s father, too.”

“You can tell me what you spoke about. Just don’t tell me where you were. I don’t want to know.”

Amelia laughed.

After they finished their food, they moved into the living room to sit on the couch. Amelia gave her impression of Kyle Spoon, and Dan gave Amelia more details about Preston Dwight’s murder that she hadn’t known.

“He was found at the park. Whoever killed him did it somewhere else and dropped the body there. He had been beaten, but the cause of death was strangulation.”

“Are you sure this wasn’t just a random act by someone who is now in, I don’t know, Chicago, doing the same thing?”

“Normally, I’d think that. But within a rolling year of Preston’s death, there wasn’t a single child murder in Gary or any of the other towns in a five-hundred-mile radius. Killers like that will seize an opportunity, and you’ll find a trail of where they’ve been. Plus, it was fall when Preston was killed. It got darker sooner. The kids were in school. Child kidnapping drops almost eighty percent when the summer months are over."

"I had no idea." Amelia was fascinated. Funny how so many killers followed a pattern they didn't even realize. She doubted any of them looked in the mirror saying, "Just three more days until the first day of summer. Kidnappin' season starts."

"Plus, the little boy was six. According to the initial report, he never went outside the home alone to look for his mother. He looked out the door, and when he saw her car, he would go out. At least that is what the mother said in her initial interview when they were looking for him. Whoever got a hold of him was someone he knew. Call it gut instinct." Dan took a deep breath. "I'm still seeing the father as the main suspect. He was a drunk. He flew into fits of jealous rage. He conveniently was asleep when the boy was taken, yet forensics say the kid was killed at that approximate time. The body was found after the detectives interviewing him let him go. That's just a little too convenient."

They spent the next half hour discussing the case together, just bouncing ideas around, then Dan stood from the couch. Smoothing out his tan pants and loosening his tie, he said he'd better start heading home.

"Why don't you just sleep here?" Amelia suggested. "The guest room never gets used. The kids won't mind as long as we ask them like adults. And I'll even make you a real breakfast in the morning if you'd like."

"How could I turn down an offer like that?" He gave Amelia that smirk that constituted a huge grin for the stoic detective.

Amelia called Adam up from the basement and Meg down from her room to meet in the family room.

"Dan said he was going to drive home, and I suggested that he just stay and use the guest room. What do you guys think?"

"Just stay in the guest room, Dan." Adam looked at both of them as if they were completely crazy to think there might be a better answer.

Everyone looked at Meg, who stood there tapping her foot with her arms folded across her chest.

"I don't know." She mused like her mother. "What's in it for me?"

"Oh, you mean on top of the free food, clothing, and shelter that you're already getting?" Amelia answered, crossing her arms over her own chest. "Hmmm...let me think. I know. A good swift kick? Soap in your mouth? A good old-fashioned spanking? Thirty days in the hole? Any one of those. You pick."

Meg couldn't keep a straight face and started to laugh.

"Hey, Dan. Could you tell me another story about your rookie days?" Meg clapped her hands together and bounced on her toes.

"Oh yeah. About the stories from your rookie days..." Amelia gave Dan that look the kids knew meant he was busted. "Maybe you're the one who needs soap in his mouth."

"You heard your mother," he grumbled. "Maybe if I tell her the story first, she'll let me know if it's appropriate."

"I can handle it, Mom. I'm not a little girl anymore, you know."

"Not much." Adam had to get in on the conversation. "That's why you still cry when you watch that stupid movie *Boys Town* with Mickey Rooney."

"That movie is not stupid." Meg gasped. "Anyone who doesn't cry when PeeWee gets hit by a car has no soul."

"I cried when PeeWee got hit by the car," Dan admitted as if confessing a serious crime.

"See?" Meg lifted her chin at her brother defiantly.

"Dan, you aren't the man I thought you were." Adam shook his head and clicked his tongue before heading back into the basement.

"Okay, then it's settled. You can stay in the guest room. But I'll warn you. In a house with only one bathroom and two teenagers, it might get a little dicey in the morning."

"I've got my weapon," Dan replied without skipping a beat.

After everyone had said their good nights and Amelia was in her room, she climbed into bed and lay awake for a short time. It was nice having Dan just down the hall. Would she have liked him to be closer? Perhaps in her room, sharing her bed? Maybe. It wasn't out of the realm of possibilities.

But it wasn't just her needs that she had to consider. Those two kids were too important to rush into anything. So far, Dan had proven to be a diamond in the rough. Meg and Adam were crazy about him. Amelia was crazy about him. But there had to be a practical side to things. Her relationship with him or any man had to be researched and studied as closely as her venture into the world of the food truck business.

But how lucky was she that this was her biggest dilemma? There were many women out in the world like Starla-Ann Dwight who loved the wrong men.

Like you didn't for a while? The thought made her shudder. The last thing Amelia wanted was to fall asleep to thoughts of her ex-husband and the mockery he'd made of her and their life together.

"Don't think about it," she mumbled.

Instead, her thoughts went to the beautiful children she had. The one thing that John had done right.

Amelia wondered if John ever thought that Adam and Meg were his greatest accomplishments, if they were the only thing he had done right. In that respect, the flabby, smart-mouthed, thickheaded

Kyle Spoon was more of a man than John would ever be.

Chapter Six

"Well, you're looking adorable today," Lila chirped as she stepped into the Pink Cupcake. "Are we being photographed again? You've been reviewed in all the magazines that count. Who is it this time?"

Amelia laughed.

"No. We aren't being reviewed again. And might I remind you that we were reviewed in the *Gary Tribune* food section and the Gary Eats section of NUVO. That paper is free. So I wouldn't say we've cracked the crust just yet."

"It's just a matter of time. If the pickle-on-a-stick people down the row can get a review in *Bon Appetit*, we certainly can." Lila pulled a bag out from her purse. "Surprise for you."

She handed the bag to Amelia.

"What?" Amelia gushed. "You shouldn't be spending your money on me."

"I'm investing in the Pink Cupcake," Lila argued, jerking her chin at the bag. "Besides, I have lots of money. If I don't spend it, the government will take it when I'm dead."

"Can you not talk about dying?"

"Hey, it happens to everyone."

"Lila. Please? One day without inviting the Grim Reaper, please?"

Shaking her head, Amelia looked in the bag and pulled out the gift Lila had bought for the truck.

"Are you kidding? Hot-pink aprons! With our logo! Lila, these are fantastic!"

"There is one for you, one for me, and two for the kids, plus an extra if we get so big we need to bring on more help."

"Meg is going to flip!" She hugged Lila tightly. "You are too good to me."

Lila hugged her back then pulled away quickly.

"Okay, enough public displays of affection. Let's get these on and start baking. Except that maybe you shouldn't, because I mean it when I say you do look very stylish this morning. What's up?"

Amelia smiled mischievously and tugged at the sides of the simple gray skirt.

"I wanted to look pretty when Dan left this morning."

Lila flopped down in the chair by the ordering window and stared.

"Oh, relax," Amelia teased her. "It isn't as scandalous as it sounds. He brought food over, and it got late while we were talking, so I invited him to stay in the guest room. End of story."

"Were the kids home?"

"Yes, we got the okay from the bosses right off the bat."

"And he stayed in the guest room the whole night?" Lila's right eyebrow rose suspiciously, and she looked at Amelia sideways.

"Of course he did."

Lila slumped as if she'd just found out she flunked a test she had studied for.

"And for that you got dressed up?"

"Lila, I'm crazy about you, but you really need to get your mind out of the gutter. I'm forty-four years old. I'm not the wild woman of Borneo anymore."

"I don't believe that," came a male voice from outside the order window.

"Who said that?" Amelia mouthed the words to Lila, who pointed toward the back of the truck.

Before she could go peek, Gavin poked his head in and gave both ladies a cheerful good morning. Amelia's stylish outfit didn't escape his attention either.

"Whoa." He smiled as he let his eyes look her up and down. "You look pretty. What, do you have a date? Some guy coming to take you out for dinner, maybe a movie or a walk in the park?"

"No." Amelia blushed.

"No? No date tonight?"

She shook her head and folded her arms over her chest.

"No. I have no plans tonight."

"Great. I'll meet you here after lock-up. I know just the place." He winked. "Don't work too hard, Lila." He grinned a grin that was irresistible, as Kyle Spoon's probably had been about five years ago.

"Never do, Gavin." Lila choked back the laughter as she stared at Amelia's shocked expression. "You walked right into that one. Didn't see the lights? Hear the bell?" She slapped the table and continued laughing.

"Oh my gosh!" Amelia started laughing herself. "Did I just get robbed? I feel like I did."

"No. You just accepted a dinner invitation from the Food Truck Alley's very own Casanova. I'm jealous."

Turning on the ovens to get them heated, both women cracked up over Gavin's straightforward manner of showing Amelia he was interested in her.

But as it got closer to lock-up time, Amelia began to get nervous.

"I don't know about this, Lila. Dan just stayed overnight last night for the very first time."

"He slept in the guest room."

"Yes, but still. That's a big step for me, and here I am already going out with another man. How do I say this? I feel a bit trampy."

"Goodness, if that makes you feel trampy, I should be calling myself the whore of Babylon," Lila mumbled.

"What did you say?" Amelia finished wiping down the ovens and flat surfaces for tomorrow's batches.

"I didn't say anything. Pay no attention to me."

"Lila, I'm asking you seriously. Should I go?"

Lila pushed a few stray red curls from her face and took both of Amelia's hands in hers.

"Yes." She smiled kindly. "Not because he's hot or because you should spread it around. But because you might need a friend to fix a flat when Dan is stuck at work. It's as simple as that. And I'll go to your house and feed your kids."

Amelia felt her nerves settle down.

"Gavin obviously likes you. It's hard not to." Lila bumped Amelia with her hip as she passed her on her way to the back door of the truck. "But that doesn't mean he calls the shots."

When she left for the night, Lila told Amelia to call her if she needed anything, like a quick exit or a place to bury the body.

While waiting for Gavin to come over, Amelia thought about what Lila had said.

She was right. Grabbing something to eat with another guy who worked the same kind of job in the same area was no big deal. She'd had lunch with him, after all. He wasn't a complete stranger.

Yeah, but that was lunch. This is dinner with wine and dark lighting.

She shook her head, trying to dislodge that voice.

"Hi." Amelia turned around to see Gavin leaning in the door. "I had one of my guys watch the place so I could run home and change. I didn't want you to feel like you were going out with a slob."

Amelia crept forward and took a look.

"My gosh." She beamed. "You look great."

Gavin was just wearing a simple pair of khakis and a black T-shirt, but he looked amazing. He had told Amelia he was in the military, and that must have been how he got his creases so perfect.

"Thanks." He nodded as if he appreciated her noticing how he had tried.

"So where are we headed?"

"Well, I hope you don't mind, but I know a great Indian restaurant just a few blocks from here."

"Are we walking there?"

"Yes, I'll lead the way."

Amelia kept the conversation going as they walked. "How was your day?"

"Actually, I had one crazy day."

"Oh yeah? What happened?"

"Well, first I got a call from the city telling me that they hadn't received my payment for my space. I told the girl that was funny because I had paid for the entire year and didn't owe anything."

"Did you talk to a girl named Jeanine?"

"How did you know?"

"She is one of two people who work in that office, and I hate to say it, but she's the smart one. You might need to go down there to get things straightened out."

"I was afraid of that. That's an all-day affair."

"Right?"

Amelia instantly felt relaxed and was ready to tell Lila she was right.

As soon as they made it to the restaurant, Amelia inhaled the sweet aroma of cilantro and heard Indian music piping through the place.

"I think they stole your decorating ideas," Gavin said, slipping his arm through Amelia's and leading her to the hostess table.

"Why do you say that?"

Gavin pointed to the banquet room just across from the restaurant's very crowded dining area. It was hot pink with gold and teal trim.

"Funny."

"What? It's a compliment."

"I'll have you know that The Pink Cupcake just acquired hot-pink aprons to match the truck."

"I bet you look amazing."

The tiny hostess, wearing a maroon sari, led them to a small table for two that was in a dark and quiet corner.

"Now, I tasted your Tex-Mex muffins, and if I could make a suggestion..."

"Please do. I don't get offended by suggestions. I just ignore them if I don't like them."

"A little more heat."

"Oh, you like things spicy. Well, I thought it could use that too, but I wanted to see if the concept would work first. I think it turned out pretty well."

"I'm amazed at some of the cupcakes you offer. So far, everything I've had has been delicious."

"I'm sorry." Amelia placed her hands in her lap as the waiter poured them some water. "I've never even tasted your Philly cheese steak sandwiches. I know. I'm a big loser. It's just that when I get to work, I'm all about the work. I usually don't even get a chance to eat throughout the day. Then I hurry home to see my kids and have dinner with them."

"I didn't say that so you'd come and try my sandwiches. I said it because it's true. And because I thought if I stopped by enough times, you'd start to talk to me. Which you did."

"Gavin, I'm just going to be blunt and up front with you." Amelia felt her heart pounding. "I think you are really nice. And you know as well as I do that you are a really good-looking guy. Please don't pretend you don't know that."

"What are you talking about? Me? Good looking? What have you been smoking, lady?"

"Stop making me laugh, or I'll never finish what I'm trying to say."

Gavin sat back and folded his arms over his wide chest. Amelia tried to finish her thought, but when she looked at his eyes, she saw he was crossing them, and she burst out laughing, making every patron in the restaurant look in her direction.

"That's it." She put her hands up. "I surrender. I'm outgunned."

Wiping her eyes with her napkin, she looked at Gavin, who was thoroughly enjoying himself.

"You have a great laugh, Amelia."

"Ask those people over there if they think so. I think I might have shattered their eardrums."

As she laid her forearm on the table, Gavin took her hand in his. He held it gently, rubbing his fingers across the top. Amelia could feel the roughness of the calluses. His skin was warm, but she pulled her hand away and tucked it back in her lap. It wasn't that she didn't want to hold his hand. She did. And, suddenly, that made her nervous.

"So, Amelia. What did you do yesterday with your free time?" he asked innocently.

Taking a deep breath, Amelia would have liked to tell him that she didn't do much. Stopped at the grocery store, put gas in the truck, you know, just the normal things.

How could she tell him that she had taken a trip to Brookhaven to visit a person she didn't know whose nephew was the strangled boy that murdered reporter was researching? He'd look at her as if she were crazy. Amelia wasn't sure she wanted Gavin to see her in that light. She wasn't sure how she wanted him to see her. So she lied.

Chapter Seven

"I've got to tell Dan."

"Tell him what?" Lila looked at Amelia as though she had grown a third eye in the middle of her forehead. "That you went out with Philly Cheese Steak Guy?"

"His name is Gavin. Can you just call him that?"

"Gavin." Lila sighed. "And you had a nice time. End of story."

"He tried to kiss me."

"But you didn't let him. You said you gave him a hug, and he kissed your cheek, and when he moved in closer, you pulled away." Lila popped a batch of blueberry cupcakes still in their batter form into the oven, closing the heavy door and pressing the timer. “Unless you didn’t pull away?”

Amelia shook her head while she looked down, concentrating on the dainty flower design she was putting on her vanilla cupcakes.

“No. I did. But I feel like that is the difference between dealing with Dan and dealing with Gavin. I lied to Gavin. He asked me what I did after work the other day, and I couldn’t tell him the truth. Only Dan would understand what I did.”

“Heavens, Amelia, what did you do?”

With a sigh, Amelia spilled the story of her visit to Brookhaven.

“Okay, perhaps that isn’t something to brag about to a possible love interest.”

“See? But Dan knows, and he understood why I did it. He wasn’t happy, but he understood. Plus, I was honest with Dan after the fact. I’m not as sure about Gavin. He works right there.” She pointed out the order window to the left where the big blue-and-silver Philly Cheese Steak truck sat. “What if things went south after he heard what I did, who I was talking to? Is it worth it?”

“Only you can decide that, honey.” Lila brushed off some flour that was on Amelia’s cheek. “What do you think Dan will say when you tell him about dinner?”

“I don’t know. I thought I’d bring it up after I went to visit Timothy Casey. That way there would be more work-related substance involved.”

“Who is Timothy Casey?” Lila squinted as if the name was familiar but she couldn’t pull up a face to go with it.

“He’s the boyfriend in the Preston Dwight case. He’s got a plumbing business over on LaPorte Road called Waterware. There’s a red-and-white sign for it. I thought I’d stop by and see what he has to say about things.”

“Yeah.” Lila snapped her fingers. “He was a suspect for a while, but they cleared him, too.” Lila nodded while she started to wipe down the counter and peeked at the cupcakes still baking.

“According to Sandra Dwight, the aunt, Timothy was the cat’s meow compared to Preston’s real father,” Amelia said.

“Really?” Lila folded up the rag she had been using and took a seat to wait for the timer. “When are you planning on doing that?”

“The kids are with their dad this weekend. I thought I’d go then.” Just as she finished her sentence, Amelia's phone began to buzz. "Speak of the devil."

John O'Malley, Amelia's ex-husband, had agreed in their divorce to take Adam and Meg a minimum of every other weekend.

John was true to his word, picking the kids up when he said he was going to and calling if there was any trouble or delay. It was a blessing and a curse. She certainly didn't want her children to suffer over the mistakes their parents had made. But she couldn't deny part of her wished he were a little more like Kyle Spoon with his crass comments and drinking problem.

As it was, John had gotten in shape after the divorce. In order for him to keep up with his twentysomething fiancée, Jennifer, it was a necessity.

But Amelia didn't feel she had let herself go. She just didn't have a gym membership or indulge in spa treatments or pay more than twenty dollars for a haircut. She kept her nails trimmed, but it had been over a year since she indulged in a manicure.

"Hello, John." She winced. John never called just to say hello or see how Adam did on a history test or if Meg helped out on the truck recently. There was always an order to be barked or a complaint to be lodged.

"Amelia. Are you having someone come to prune the oak that's on the southern side of your house?"

"What? Not that I know of." She pinched her brow and searched her memory for such a request. Nope. Nothing rang a bell.

"I just got a call from Daryl Limski. He said that he drove past your place and the branches of the oak were getting too close to the roof on the southern side of the house."

"And?"

"And, Amelia, that can cause damage to the gutters and the shingling of the house. If you have to pay for those repairs yourself, that can cost anywhere from four thousand to six thousand dollars."

"Okay, John. I'm at work right now, and worrying about branches and gutters just isn't on my radar. Do you remember how you used to act when I'd call you at work to tell you the dryer was on the fritz or the tile in the bathroom was cracked?"

"When you called me at work, I was busy."

Amelia's blood ignited, and she felt the string of swears rising up in her throat. But she wouldn't say them. Clearing her throat, she stroked the nape of her neck and took a deep breath.

"Unless it's an emergency, John, I need you to stop calling me at work. I'll talk to Mr. Mezenio, the landlord, and let him know your concern. Until then, tell Daryl Limski to quit spying and mind his own business."

"Calm down, Amelia. Don't get all excited over nothing. You can never take any kind of criticism."

"Good-bye, John. The kids will see you Friday."

Amelia growled as soon as she hit the disconnect button. Why didn't John ever ask what she did in her off time? She'd love to see the expression on his face after telling him she was visiting people not only at their Brookhaven residence, but also at a Brookhaven corner tavern. What would Daryl Limski do if he saw that? The thought made her smile.

"That went well." Lila patted Amelia's hand over the counter.

"Lila, what am I doing even worrying about Dan and Gavin? John can call and talk to me for thirty seconds, and I'm ready to take a chainsaw to any man who comes within twenty feet of me."

"You worry because, despite what John thinks he knows, you are a wonderful person who cares about other people and their feelings. Only someone special would go into Brookhaven to talk to a stranger in an attempt to ease their pain. Your ex-husband doesn't know you. And it's driving him crazy."

"I hope you're right about the driving-him-crazy part. Every little bit helps."

The women laughed just as the timer for the oven went off. A second batch of vanilla cupcakes was ready for decorating. Although Lila had learned quite a bit about the art of mixing ingredients and balancing the books, she left the real artwork to Amelia.

Each was decorated with care and love. So much so that Mother Mary could come down from Heaven and indulge in any one of the confectionaries, assuming its perfection was on display especially for her. But it was Amelia's signature. The cupcakes weren't just delicious with unique flavors—they were pretty. The newspapers that reviewed The Pink Cupcake called them works of art for the eyes and taste buds.

It may not have seemed like much to John. Nothing she did ever seemed like much to him. But to Amelia, the big hot-pink truck, the matching T-shirts and aprons, the whole wild scene of Food Truck Alley was beautiful.

So when John came and picked up the kids after school on Friday, she was more than happy to stay in the house when he pulled up after getting the truck washed and waxed to a blinding sparkle.

She kissed Adam and Meg, told them to be good and do their homework, then shut the door behind them, listening for the doors on John's car to slam shut and the sound of the engine pulling out of the driveway and driving away.

She let her shoulders relax and slid her feet across the tiled floor into the kitchen. There, she poured herself a glass of wine and sat down in front of her laptop to do a little research on Timothy Casey. From what she could gather about him on Facebook and his business website, Sandra Dwight was spot on when she said he was a good guy.

His business website for plumbing and bathroom remodeling boasted satisfactory reviews from almost one hundred customers who claimed he handled their plumbing problem promptly and professionally and that his prices were reasonable. His showroom featured fancy copper piping along with elegant sinks, toilets, sunken bathtubs, and showers that sported five strategically placed showerheads so every shower could be like a spa treatment.

“Too bad I don’t have any plumbing problems,” Amelia said.

She scanned his Facebook page. There were posts relating to a birthday party for an alderman from some neighborhood Amelia wasn’t familiar with. There were pictures of a man who Amelia could guess was Casey laughing while leaning into a firefighter, both of them holding beers in what looked like a party at the station.

“Firefighters celebrate Station #270 Historic Landmark Status.” Amelia took a sip of wine as she read the article. According to the reporter, Tim Casey helped get the building researched and registered as a historic building and also listed as one of the most distinguished landmarks in Gary.

“How many landmarks does Gary have?”

Amelia continued to read.

Timothy did a lot of work with the VA Hospital. He organized the local motorcycle club's Toys for Tots drive every Christmas season. He golfed, knew karate, and when he wasn't working or organizing some event, he was hanging out at home, working out with his two pit bulls, Rosie and Max.

"No mention of a wife or fiancée. No mention of children." Amelia leaned in to the screen and squinted. A few years ago, Timothy Casey might have looked slightly different. He might have had a little more hair, and maybe he was a little harder around the middle. But he wasn't that handsome. He wasn't ugly but rather plain. Certainly he was no match for Kyle Spoon in the looks department. But judging by all the pictures with friends, Amelia thought Timothy must have made up for it in personality. From where she was sitting, he looked as if he were playing the part of the king of the prom.

"Well, this might not be so bad."

She planned to stop by the business and ask a plumbing question. Simple enough, right? People did that, didn't they? Or maybe they called first?

"No. The element of surprise is better," she assured herself.

Chapter Eight

The following morning, Amelia woke up to a bright sun shining in her room and nothing but quiet. She loved her kids, but there was something about waking up to a completely quiet house that she savored. Stretching in her bed, she looked at the clock. It wasn't even eight o'clock yet on her day off.

The Pink Cupcake had been doing so well that there were a few Saturdays during the past few months that she didn't have to be at her usual spot next to the Philly Cheese Steak truck. Today, she was especially glad of that.

After sleeping on it, she thought maybe Lila was right. She hadn't done anything to be ashamed of. She just went to dinner with another person, and when that person tried to kiss her, she stopped it. Nothing happened.

As she thought about it, Amelia felt the webs of confusion forming again, and her thoughts were getting all gummed up in them.

"Come on!" she yelled to the empty house. "You're not in high school. It's no big deal!" With a grunt and a sigh, she pulled herself out of bed, hit the shower, got dressed, and went downstairs to make a cup of coffee.

She opened her laptop, to the same web page of a grinning Timothy Casey staring back at her. Without overthinking it, Amelia grabbed her purse, locked the front door, climbed into her trusty sedan, and started the engine. A new car would be needed soon. If sales continued the way they were going for a little while longer, there might be an opportunity to upgrade. She could practically hear Adam's argument as to why he should inherit the sedan. He could run errands for her. He could drive Meg to school. What if there was some kind of emergency?

Shaking her head, she decided she'd cross that bridge when she got to it. For now, she had to keep her eyes open for Waterware.

The stretch of this road was industrial, with a couple of block-shaped buildings supporting smokestacks that waved gray silken scarves of smoke out the top.

The parking lots were full since these factories operated twenty-four hours a day. Wedged in between the factories were a few businesses.

Shapiro's Deli was one. That had to make a killing every day since it was the only lunch place around aside from the McDonald's two blocks over and a 7-11 convenience store at the end of the block.

A currency exchange was next to the deli. That place probably had a line a mile long every payday. Beside it was an empty unit with a For Rent sign in the window.

Finally, stretching across two units was the sign that read Waterware. Showcased in the window was a giant copper bathtub, an elegant sink that looked as if it was sitting on a stone pedestal, the bowl made of green glass that looked like leaves, and a shower stall like the one on the website that had jets coming from six angles.

As she parked her car, Amelia wondered if she shouldn't have dressed up to pay Mr. Casey a visit. She hated to admit it, but sometimes it helped to look her best when trying to get information out of a man.

When she approached the door, she noticed a little sign that read Please Ring Bell, and she did just that.

Within seconds, a young woman with blond hair and a grumpy expression came to the door. She yanked it open as if it were the last thing in the world she wanted to do.

"Hi. Do you have an appointment?"

"No, I'm sorry. I don't. Is Timothy Casey in today?"

"Yeah. Just have a seat. I'll get him."

Amelia smiled and sat down on a hard wooden bench that faced the showroom.

Along the wall across from her were dozens of showerheads of all shapes, sizes, and colors. At the other end of the room, there were toilets and bidets that looked like exotic porcelain sculptures. A row of custom shower stalls lined the back wall, and throughout the showroom floor were tubs and sinks with their own unique faucets that screamed expensive.

She noticed the wall of bizarre metal racks. She caught a glimpse of the hanging price tag and almost choked. Twelve hundred dollars? For electric towel warmers?

Amelia shook her head. Could she ever see herself buying such a thing? Even if she had twelve hundred dollars to throw around, this would have to be at the bottom of her list, right after voluntary root canal.

This setup was certainly not what she had in mind when she heard the word *plumber*.

“Who is it?” Amelia heard a male voice from around the corner in what she assumed was an office.

“I don’t know.” It was the voice of the grump who opened the door.

“Did you ask?”

“I asked if she had an appointment. She said no.”

A chair scraped. There was some mumbling, then suddenly, the man Amelia had seen smiling and laughing on Facebook appeared.

“Hi. I’m Tim Casey. Can I help you?”

“Amelia Harley. I’m sorry. I didn’t realize that I needed an appointment.”

“No, it’s okay. What can I do for you?”

"Well, I wanted to ask you a couple of questions. Can we talk in your office?"

"Sure. Are you looking to have some remodeling done?"

"Not exactly." Amelia followed behind Tim until he stretched out his hand, indicating where his office was.

Amelia stepped inside and was shocked at the difference between the office and the rest of the showroom. Papers were scattered all over the desk in multiple piles that looked as if they hadn't been touched in months. Pieces of plumbing were on the floor. Copper piping of various sizes, a couple showerheads, plastic zip ties, three plungers, and a drain snake were scattered around an old-fashioned olive-green file cabinet.

There were photos all over the walls of Tim at a golf course, at restaurants, and holding plaques, shaking hands and smiling in each and every one. He knew people. Even the late Mayor Pearl was standing next to him in one of them.

The desk Tim sat behind was a huge metal monstrosity like the nuns used to have at Amelia's grade school when she was growing up. It was a metal behemoth that, once settled in a spot, wasn't ever going to move again.

"I was hoping you might be able to tell me about the night Preston Dwight was killed."

Amelia waited for Tim to stop and either glare at her or slip into a melancholy state at the mention of the name. Instead, she got blindsided.

"Who?"

That was an odd response.

"Preston Dwight. He was Starla-Ann Dwight's son, who was murdered about ten years ago." Amelia took a seat in one of the chairs in front of the desk. Tim walked around the desk and plunked down in his seat with a grunt.

"Miss Harley, right? Would you like a cup of coffee?"

"No, thanks." She smiled patiently. "Do you remember anything about that night, Mr. Casey?"

"Call me Tim." He rubbed his chin, the stubbly whiskers making a scratchy noise. "I know you aren't a cop, Miss Harley, because I know every uniform in Gary plus half the surrounding towns." He folded his hands and leaned forward on his desk.

"I didn't say I was a cop." She smiled and blinked her eyes innocently. "I spoke with Sandra Dwight, Starla-Ann's sister. She mentioned what a great guy you were to her sister. You seemed to make an impression on her."

Tim snapped his fingers.

"Dwight. Yes." He slapped his forehead. "I'm so sorry, Miss Harley. I guess you could say I get around, and sometimes a name just doesn't register at first." He waved a lazy hand around his head. "Yes, I remember Starla-Ann. We dated for a while. But the death of her son, well, jeez, that just sort of put an end to things between us."

"Please, call me Amelia. There seems to be a consensus that the boy's father, Kyle Spoon, was responsible. Do you think that's true?"

"I think it's completely possible. The man had a drinking problem and a temper. Not to mention his life seemed to be speeding quickly in no particular direction. I'd had more than one confrontation with him."

"Really? What about...if you don't mind my asking?"

"Over Starla-Ann and Preston. I guess he thought being a bad father was better than me being the boy's father."

"You and Starla were that serious?"

"Absolutely. But there's only so much baggage a man can take on. Once Preston was gone, Starla-Ann just couldn't function. I wanted to help her. But she just sort of slipped away. Plus, with Kyle walking around free, it was a daily reminder of what he'd done to her son. It was just sad."

"Yeah, it really is. Why do you think the police never arrested Kyle?"

"I couldn't tell you that. But a guy like that knows the system. He knows how to slip through the cracks. I'm sure they all knew it was him but couldn't pin it down. Like he was the O. J. Simpson of Gary." Tim chuckled at his own comment. "If I ever saw the guy again, I'd have plenty to say to him."

Amelia leaned forward. "I'll bet you would." She nodded, but strangely, her gut was twisting a little inside. "Tim, did you speak to a guy named David Scranton at all? He was the reporter looking into Preston's case recently. Maybe you heard about him on the news? He was found murdered in a motel."

Tim furrowed his brows in thought then shook his head.

"No. I don't recall ever talking to anyone by that name." He began to chuckle. "I guess I'm just too busy to keep on top of local news."

"Well, I think I've taken up enough of your time." Amelia stood from her chair and leaned forward, her hand extended. "I really appreciate you talking to me."

Tim shook her hand. His palm was sweaty.

"Do you live in Gary, Amelia?"

"I do. I remember when the story about Preston's death happened. My boy was the same age at the time."

"Well, here." He handed her a business card. "If you ever need any plumbing work done, please give me a call. We do remodeling, but we also provide regular plumbing services, too."

"Thanks, Tim. I'll do that."

Tim walked Amelia to the door and held it open for her as she walked out. She could feel his eyes on her as she made her way to her car and wondered if he was looking because she was a woman or if there was another reason.

Amelia hadn't realized her hands had been clenched into fists until she reached for her car door and climbed in, immediately locking the doors again once she was safely behind the wheel.

She slipped on her sunglasses as she looked back at the door, but Tim was gone.

Chapter Nine

"That was weird," she told the steering wheel. Tim was a nice-enough guy. She didn't think there was anything particularly creepy about him. Something just felt odd. A guy who was not only a witness to the devastating effects of a child murder but also a person of interest in that murder forgot the name of the victim? He was either in the early stages of Alzheimer's or lying.

Plus, the story of Scranton's death was in the paper. Between all his friends and clients, he would have heard about it. Especially since Tim was associated with the cold case. People talked in Gary.

Amelia's stomach grumbled.

"That's it. I'm not thinking straight. I'm hungry." She contemplated going to

Shapiro's Deli but decided to go on an adventure to find something else.

She took a different route toward home and found herself at Wolf Road, where the No-Tell Motel was. It was practically walking distance from Waterware.

"Now that is a weird coincidence."

Amelia made a split-second decision and turned in to the parking lot. She shut off her engine, got out, and headed toward the part of the building with the neon sign that read O-F-F-I-C-E.

Inside, she saw the man who had been questioned by the uniformed officer the other day. He was wearing a Hawaiian shirt and baggy jeans, and his feet were exposed in a pair of flip-flops. The little bell over the door rang when she went in. He turned his bulldog face in her direction but immediately changed his demeanor when he saw Amelia walk in.

"Hi." He waved cheerfully as if he'd been expecting her. "Nice afternoon out there. I sure wish I wasn't stuck in here."

His friendly demeanor didn't fit his appearance at all. *Never judge a book.*

Amelia smiled but still got the feeling his friendliness was a little forced.

"Hi. I'd like a room."

The manager nodded and looked Amelia up and down.

"Would you like our hourly nap, or is this for overnight?" It was the No-Tell Motel, and Amelia was sure there was *no telling* what was going on in some of the rooms. There was no telling what she was going to do, but she couldn't ignore the fact that the place popped up in front of her like a lightning bolt.

"Just a nap. That sounds perfect."

"Okay. Cash or charge?"

"Cash." Surprisingly, the manager did his job with very little concern with what she was there for. He pulled out a small paper receipt, scribbled some information on it in barely legible script, and tore off the top copy to hand to her.

"That'll be $35 dollars for two hours. Anything over six hours gets charged the overnight fee."

"Okay."

As Amelia felt around for her wallet in her purse, she took a quick glance around the room and saw that there were cameras strategically placed in the corners: one aimed at the door, the other at the counter. On one side sat an old brown couch that didn't look very comfortable, sandwiched between two end tables.

She handed over the cash, realizing she would not be treating herself to a special "kids are gone so treat yourself " dinner of sushi or Moody's burgers. It would be leftover chili or maybe peanut butter and jelly.

Suppressing a sigh, she watched the manager put the money in a lock box behind the counter and lift a key off a corkboard with half a dozen other keys.

"Number nine. Just out this door, to the left, second from the end on the first level. Enjoy your stay."

"Thanks." Amelia took the key and left the office in search of her room.

Suddenly, she wondered if Dan had already viewed the surveillance tapes from the hotel. If he hadn't and they recorded several days at a time, he might see her on here and wonder what was going on. And then if she told him about her dinner with Gavin, he might think the absolute worst.

"You can't do anything about it now," she mumbled, looking at the windows of all the other units that were pulled tightly shut.

Finally, she reached room number nine. She slipped the key in the lock and opened the door. It smelled of disinfectant and cigarettes.

She shut the door behind her and peeked out the window. No one was peeking back. There weren't any parted curtains quickly falling back into place. There weren't any strangers walking out of their doors to check out her car or stare at the closed door to unit number nine.

It was almost depressing how absolutely no one paid any attention to anyone else. But that was the appeal of the No-Tell Motel, she supposed. It was not surprising that there were no witnesses. Amelia didn't think it was an honor-among-thieves scenario. She was convinced no one came forward with information about David Scranton's murder because no one saw anything, plain and simple.

She dropped her purse on a table and walked around the room. The carpet was an odd rust color that was worn down from years and years of people walking over the same path.

The bedspread was of a scratchy fabric printed with blue and brown leaves found nowhere in nature. The walls were paneled. There was a huge dresser across from the bed and a television bolted securely to the wall above it.

Nothing was coming to her. She had just spent thirty-five dollars to sit in a stinky room for five minutes and had come up with not one single idea of why she was there, what could have happened to David Scranton, or how it tied to Preston Dwight.

She stood up and went to the bathroom. It had white tiles, and the bleach smell was very strong. A thin gray shower curtain hung across the tub, and Amelia instinctively pulled it aside. Too many horror movies caused her to do that. A crazy person or a monster usually lurked behind a closed shower curtain. But all Amelia found was a white tub with rust around the drain.

She turned to the little sink and turned the cold-water lever. A small drizzle of water came out. It was enough to fill her hands for her to splash her face. It was the least she could do to feel refreshed.

She didn't even want to touch the towels to dry off. Even the toilet paper was a better option, so she pulled a wad off and dabbed around her eyes and around her chin. She didn't see a trash can, so she tossed the paper into the toilet and flushed.

The water swirled around, but the paper didn't go down. In fact, it kept swirling, and the water continued to rise.

"No," Amelia ordered. The water didn't listen. "No. No. No!"

It rose and surged over the edge of the bowl like a miniature waterfall covering the floor and spreading toward the door and the ugly rust-colored carpet.

"No! I'm not paying for this." She grabbed the raggedy towel and dropped it in front of the water to stop the advancement at least for a few minutes while she grabbed the key to the room and ran out to the motel office.

"Hello," the manager said, forcing that odd smile again as if he were thrilled Amelia had come back.

"Hi. The toilet in my room overflowed."

His eyebrows immediately arched, and his face took on even more of an appearance of a bulldog being scolded.

"The toilet? Oh no. I'm so sorry. Good thing we have our plumber right down the street." He picked up his cell phone and made a call. "Hey, Tim. It's Ivan. Can you stop by? I've got a toilet overflow." Ivan looked at Amelia, giving her a quick wink. "Thanks, buddy. Sure. I can move the occupant. No. That's fine. I appreciate it."

He hung up his phone and looked at Amelia.

"The plumber for the building is just down the street. He'll be here in twenty minutes or so."

Amelia swallowed.

"Oh, how convenient. Is that the Waterware place I drove past on my way here?"

"It is." Ivan's face lit up. "I've known the owner for years. He handles all my units here. He does a good job. This is an old building. He'll fix the toilet in that room. If you don't mind, I'll move you to another unit."

"That would be fine." Amelia nodded, looked at her watch, and then smiled at Ivan.

"Let's see. Lucky number eighteen." He took off another key and gave it to Amelia, who quickly handed him back the key to number nine.

"Here you go." She smiled. "So the plumber can get in."

Ivan nodded and smiled back. Without another word, Amelia turned and walked out of the office, hurrying toward the door with the number eighteen on it. Once inside, she locked the door along with the chain.

She peeked out the window. Fortunately, she could see the entire parking lot, as well as unit number nine.

True to his word, within twenty minutes, Tim Casey pulled up outside the motel office in a white van with Waterware Plumbing and Remodeling printed in red letters on the side.

He pulled into a vacant spot just a stone's throw from her room. As he climbed out, he popped open the back of the van, and Amelia could see the interior. It was as messy and cluttered as his office had been, minus all the photographs.

Don't know anything about David Scranton? Really? How could he possibly not know about the murder here? How could that be? She squinted, trying to see without being seen herself. When Tim went inside,

Amelia grabbed a chair from the little table in the room and made herself comfortable.

Tim emerged again from the office, twirling a key on his finger, when he suddenly stopped. He stopped in front of Amelia's car. Looking at it, he looked around.

Without thinking, Amelia leaned back into the shadows and held her breath. Through the sheer panel curtain, she watched Tim look across the lot at every unit as if looking for something. Or someone. Peeking through the tiniest crack, not daring to cause the slightest motion in the curtains, Amelia watched.

"He is looking for me."

Chapter Ten

Tim shook his head then continued walking, letting himself into unit nine. Amelia couldn't leave. She didn't dare risk running into him in the parking lot. But it was clear to her that he was hiding something.

"But what? A successful guy with all his connections and friends, why would he lie?" Amelia held her breath and waited.

Staring at the truck, Amelia studied all the things that were in the back. From where she was sitting, she could see black tubing and white tubing. There were some hanging light fixtures, probably for finding leaks in crawlspaces and basements. There were half a dozen spray cans of WD-40 and, of course, several plungers. There were also some odd things in there. A portable generator stuck out. A hair dryer. A fire extinguisher. A vacuum cleaner.

When Tim emerged again, he walked to the back of the truck, grabbed a plunger and a wild contraption that had to be some kind of drain snake especially made for a toilet, and headed back into the unit.

Looking at her watch, Amelia wondered how long this would take. It wasn't as if she had any particular place to go, but she didn't want to stay where she was, recalling how Tim had stared and watched her as she walked to her car. It was just a plain sedan, but right now it might as well have had red-and-purple flames along the sides with Amelia Harley's Ride spray-painted across the hood.

It was another fifteen minutes before he came out of unit nine, closing the door behind him and strolling back to the office. He paid no attention to her car this time. It was another ten minutes before he got back in his van, revved the engine, and tore out of the parking lot as if the devil were chasing him.

"Must be a real plumbing emergency." Amelia sighed. Stretching her arms over her head, Amelia stood, unlocked the door, and left it open, leaving the door key sitting on the table.

"I'm not coming back to this place. And I'm not going to worry about key-returning etiquette."

With her keys in her hand, she quickly walked to her car, climbed in, and started the engine. She wouldn't feel safe until she was back in her house.

As she began to back out, her phone chirped in her pocket, making her jump. Thankfully, it was Dan. She answered with a breathless hello as she pulled onto Wolf Road.

"You sound out of breath. Are you exercising?"

"No." What could she say? Just a white lie. A tiny white lie. "I'm just running some errands, and I jogged to hold the door for some pregnant lady."

Where in the world that concoction had come from, Amelia couldn't say, but it was good enough. Dan seemed to buy it.

"Oh, well, since you did your good deed for the day, how about I treat you to lunch at Moody's. I don't have a lot of time, but I get an hour for lunch. It's the law."

Amelia giggled.

"That sounds great. How about I meet you there?"

"See you in half an hour."

The line went dead. Amelia dropped the phone in her lap to drive and headed in the direction of Moody's. It would take her about that long to get there if traffic held up. When she looked ahead, things seemed clear.

When she checked her rearview mirror, she saw a familiar white truck quickly approaching. She gripped the steering wheel, trying to watch behind her and the road ahead of her at the same time.

"Get a hold of yourself, Amelia. There are white work trucks all over the place. The chances of that being Tim Casey are..."

She tried to nonchalantly get a look at the driver, but he kept his vehicle close enough to perhaps be following her but far enough away she couldn't get a good look at the driver.

"It's not him," she said out loud. "I'm being paranoid. I'll just get where I'm going. Dan will be at Moody's." She hit the gas and quickly sped down Harrison Boulevard, cutting over to Montrose, and finally on

Ashland Avenue. She pulled into Moody's parking lot, slipping quickly into a spot next to Dan's car. The van didn't seem to be in sight.

Thank goodness Dan was already here.

Stepping out of his car, Dan appeared to Amelia like a guardian angel. His beige suit and brown beat walkers normally made Amelia's heart skip a beat. Today, she got out of her car and nearly ran up to him.

She looked back to the street. A white van drove past. The driver wore sunglasses, and he seemed to be looking at her.

Was he Tim Casey? Or was she just being paranoid again? The van drove away and disappeared.

"What's the matter?" Dan asked.

"Nothing." She stood on her tiptoes to kiss Dan's cheek. "Just happy to see you. I'm starved. Let's go in."

As usual, Dan's face set off a flurry of hellos and how are yas from the staff. Amy, Dan's favorite waitress and special friend, was there to give them a quiet seat in the main dining room near the fireplace, which was dark and cold for now.

“She’ll have the Italian sub. I’ll have a po’boy,” Dan said, his face serious and calm like always.

“Mixing it up a little, huh, Detective,” Amy said playfully. “I’ll get these for you right away.”

“Thanks, Amy.” Dan leaned back in his seat and looked at Amelia. She had her hands casually on the table, and he took one of them in his. Immediately, she flashed back to her dinner with Gavin. But she didn’t pull her hand away from Dan. She squeezed his hand affectionately.

Amelia wanted to tell him about Tim, but she only had a gut feeling, not proof. Not yet. Would Dan be able to help if she told him? She decided to hold off until she could think things through.

“So, any news with the David Scranton case?” Amelia tilted her head to the left. Her confession would have to wait.

Dan loosened his tie.

“I’ve got something here I’d like you to take a look at.”

Amelia straightened in her seat, folded her hands in front of her, and leaned forward.

"But I have to warn you. It's disturbing."

She tilted her head to the left again as Dan withdrew an envelope from inside his jacket.

"Is that a crime scene photo?" She couldn't hold back the eagerness in her voice. It was macabre and dark, yet Amelia was very interested to see it. She was curious, and for Dan to let her in on this tiny bit of information showed that he not only trusted her, but valued her opinion.

"It's two. One of the boy, Preston Dwight. Another of David Scranton."

Amelia's eyes bugged, and she held her breath as he slid the photos across the table to her.

She put her hand over her mouth.

The photo of Preston Dwight thankfully did not reveal his whole face. There was his neck, his chin, and his lower lip. The boy's skin was not just pale, but gray.

"You see the mark around his neck?" Dan whispered.

Reluctantly leaning closer to the photo, Amelia trained her eyes on that small detail and nodded. "Have you ever seen anything like that before?"

The indentation around Preston's small throat was oddly patterned.

"Now, I've seen rope markings. I've seen nylon stocking markings. I've seen more than I care to admit. But I couldn't tell you what made that marking. If I found that, I'd have an idea of the murder weapon used on Preston and..."

Dan pulled out the other image and placed it on top.

"David Scranton."

In this second photo, David Scranton's whole face was visible. His eyes stared out, forever seeing the image of his killer. He was in the bathtub with his shirt on. The sleeves had been sloppily rolled up, and his wrists had been cut to make it look as if he had tried to commit suicide.

The bathroom layout was all too familiar. In fact, Amelia began to panic that perhaps it was the very room she had just been in. That could be room number nine or room number eighteen.

"This is a stupid question, but you're sure he didn't kill himself, right?"

Amelia had to say something. She had to bring herself back into the present, at Moody's restaurant, sitting across the table from Detective Dan Walishovsky. Otherwise, she was afraid she might faint.

"If you look at the crime scene, you'll see there is very little blood. Almost none. If it were a real suicide attempt, that white tile floor would be red." Dan's voice was steady, like a professor teaching an intro to forensics. "But look at his neck."

Squaring herself, Amelia looked.

"That's the same weird marking as Preston had, all right."

Amy arrived with a plate in each hand.

"Hope you guys are hungry. Detective, I told them to add a few slices of raw onion and an extra pickle slice for you."

"You're going to make some man very happy someday, Amy," Dan quipped, allowing Amelia enough time to flip the crime scene photos over and pull them onto her lap.

"You guys enjoy your lunch." Amy winked at Amelia before she walked away.

Amelia looked at her favorite Italian sub sandwich and was afraid some of her appetite might have left her. Dan, unfazed by the images in the photos, dug right in.

"Well, I can tell you." Amelia picked up her sandwich, the smell of salami, pecorinos, and vinegar enticing her empty stomach. "I've never seen anything that would make a mark like that. Two lines with a squiggly line down the middle?"

Wiping his lips with a paper napkin, Dan shook his head.

"Sometimes a fresh set of eyes helps move things along."

"Sorry, I don't know." Amelia took a bite of her sandwich. "This is so good."

Dan stopped chewing and looked at Amelia with a very devilish grin on his face.

"If I didn't know that you were a baker during the day, I'd swear you were a seasoned homicide detective."

"What?" she asked with a mouth full of food.

"Only a real detective can look at crime scene photos one minute then eat a meal the next. You surprise me, Amelia. All the time."

It was a wonderful compliment. Amelia flashed back to all the times she tried to talk to her ex-husband about his work and how he would condescendingly explain something as simple as a subpoena or filing a motion. But that was because he was too busy explaining his unhappy marriage to a twenty-five-year-old. The guy had to be exhausted.

As she took another bite, Amelia quickly pushed her ex-husband from her mind.

"So what is your next step?"

"We're looking into the three main suspects that were named in the paper."

"Well, Starla-Ann is dead." Amelia took a sip of water from the glass Amy brought for her "Remember, I told you that." Peeking up at Dan playfully, she squeezed his hand.

"Yes, your detective work is to be commended." He snickered. "But that doesn't mean we don't still look into it. Did she have a guilty conscience?"

"I don't know about that. I don't think so. She wasn't much, but I think she loved her little boy. I think I agree with her sister. She died of a broken heart."

Dan nodded, but his expression didn't change.

"I know. I know. But it was her sister. What was she supposed to say? Not all mothers are like you, Amelia. I hate to tell you how many are the complete opposite. When the world dealt you lemons, you turned around and made some lemonade cupcakes that put your little hot-pink truck on the map and some food on the table to boot."

Amelia blinked as she tried to keep the blush from her cheeks.

"You are a good mother, a truly good mother. I think it's against your DNA to think there might be women out there who have no right to have any kids."

"I just don't think that was Starla-Ann. I think she was poor and maybe a little stupid. But I don't think she was evil. Not like that."

Amelia took another bite. She sure was hungry.

"Lemonade cupcakes?" Dan said. "That sounds delicious. Do you make those sometimes?"

They finished their food, with Dan insisting on paying the tab, and walked back out to the parking lot, where Amelia quickly scanned the lot and the street for the white Waterware van. There was nothing even close to that. She had nothing to worry about. *You're being paranoid*, she told herself again.

"I guess you're headed back to the station," Amelia said.

"Yep."

"Do you want to come over this evening for dinner? The kids won't be there, so my house will be clean and quiet. I can try making some lemonade cupcakes."

He patted his stomach and tugged his pants. "I'm not going to be able to chase the bad guys if I keep eating your cupcakes."

"Oh, I doubt that very much." Tilting her chin up, she waited for Dan to lean forward and kiss her. She could feel his chest and stomach beneath his button-down shirt and jacket, and there was nothing meaty about it.

She felt safe standing so close to him. As if she were hiding from the rain underneath a mighty oak tree. When his lips touched hers, Amelia quickly inhaled to smell the spicy scent of his cologne.

He slipped one arm around her waist, and she certainly felt the muscles there as she easily eased into him. When Dan pulled back, looking at her with that twinkle in his eye without smiling or speaking, Amelia spilled her secret. One of them.

"Dan, I went to dinner with Gavin." As soon as she said it, she wished she hadn't.

"Who's Gavin?" Dan stepped back and pulled his arm slowly from around her waist.

"He's the guy who runs the Philly Cheese Steak truck next to mine. It didn't mean anything. I spent most of the night talking about the kids and work." She tugged at the strap of her purse over her shoulder.

"Is this someone you are interested in?" Dan put both his hands in his pockets and watched Amelia's face.

"Not like I am with you." She looked out to the street and sighed. There was no way she would tell him about her hunch regarding Tim Casey. Not after she opened her big mouth spilling the beans about Gavin, who was a nothing, a nobody in her life. Why didn't she listen to Lila?

Dan stared down at Amelia then looked at his watch.

"I've got to get back to the station."

"Would you come over when you're done tonight? We can talk." Then she saw it again, the white Waterware truck. It drove past the parking lot as if it was on its way somewhere. But Amelia wasn't so sure of that. She wanted to grab Dan by the lapel, shake him, point to the van, and tell him the man driving was Timothy Casey and he was following her because she had caught him in a lie about Preston Dwight and David Scranton and the No-Tell Motel. But that would mean something else she was keeping from him, another secret and a dangerous one.

More dangerous than going for dinner with the handsome and persistent Gavin? Really? She shook her head and focused on the issue at hand. Besides, the white truck was already gone.

"I'll call you."

"Okay." Amelia pulled her keys from her pocket, opened the driver's-side door, and slid in behind the wheel. Without looking back, she started the engine and waited for Dan to get in his car and drive away first. But he didn't. Instead, he came around and knocked on the window.

"What do you want? License and registration?"

Dan chuckled, the left corner of his mouth curling up slightly.

"Amelia, there are certain things I need to keep from you out of necessity due to my line of work. You know this. Yet you still trust me. It would only be the gentlemanly thing for me to extend you the same courtesy."

"You're not mad at me?"

"No." Dan shook his head. "I'm a sucker for a pretty face."

"You are sweeter than sugar."

"That's what I've been told." Tossing his keys in his hand, Dan turned and walked to his car. He leaned down at the passenger-side window, and Amelia immediately rolled it down.

"I don't think I'll be able to stop by tonight. But tomorrow for sure. When will the kids be back? I'd like to see them, too." At that moment, Amelia saw Dan in a completely different light. She almost started to cry.

Blinking her eyes to keep any tears back, she grinned.

"They'll be home around four o'clock."

"I should be able to get there around three." Dan tapped the hood of Amelia's car then climbed into his. With a honk, he waved, pulled out of the driveway, and headed in the direction of the police station.

Amelia backed out and headed in the direction of home, her head twisting and turning as if it were on a swivel as she looked for any white van that might be following her. There was nothing. Or at least there was nothing that she could see.

Chapter Eleven

Business on Monday at the Pink Cupcake was jumping.

Amelia flew back and forth from oven to oven without a break for the entire morning rush. Lila had money in her hand, either taking it or giving change until the cash box seemed as if it were going to burst.

Finally, the crowd settled down, and each of them grabbed a bottle of water and flopped down to rest their feet before they started getting ready for the lunchtime rush.

"I don't know why you told him about Gavin." Lila shook her head after hearing Amelia's confession.

"It just came out, Lila. I can't keep anything from him. Well, not anything like that. I can spare him the details of my morning rituals and bathroom habits, but not that."

"You did tell him nothing happened and that it was just dinner."

"Yeah."

"And…"

Tightness settled into Amelia's chest, and she felt the sting of tears in her eyes.

"What?" Lila stood and went to Amelia, putting her hand on her shoulder. "Did he call it quits? If he did, I'll have words for him. So harsh he'll need a dictionary to figure out how I insulted him."

"No." Amelia wiped her eyes. "No. In fact, he was a prince. He came over yesterday to see me and because he wanted to see the kids." She sniffled. "He wanted to see my kids, Lila. What kind of a great guy is he?"

Lila smiled and folded her arms over her chest, wiggling her red-polished nails. She nodded, making her red curls bounce and her dangly earrings jingle.

"We all ate together, and they sat on the couch while I got the food ready. Lila, just listening to them talking was so awesome.

And between you and me, I'd never tell them this, but Dan listened to everything they said as if he were their father. In fact, he was better than John ever was."

"Do you think you see that kind of future for the two of you?"

"I don't know. But I know that Dan is not a man to just take for granted."

The morning rush had launched the Pink Cupcake into hyper-drive. Just as Amelia and Lila got the first batch of cupcakes out of the oven and decorated, there was a line forming outside the window. The lunchtime crowd seemed twice the size of the breakfast crowd, and that nearly wiped them out.

The peanut-butter-and-jelly cupcakes sold out first. Then the peach-ginger cupcakes were gobbled up. Surprisingly, there were about half a dozen double chocolate cupcakes still left as the afternoon crowd finally started to dwindle away.

"I am exhausted." Lila stretched her arms over her head. "I think this has been our best day yet."

She immediately began to work on the receipts, adding up the totals and separating the cash from the charges and making a list of what it cost to operate that day.

"I wonder if the other trucks had as busy of a day or if there was just a desperate need for sweets today?" Amelia flopped down on her seat at the back of the truck, leaning over and stretching her arms to shut off the last oven.

After looking out the front order window, Lila jerked her head back in and whispered loudly, "Don't know. But I do know there is someone coming to see you who is probably hoping for something sweet."

Looking out the window, Amelia saw Gavin's salt-and-peppered head bobbing along as he came to the back entrance.

"Knock, knock." He peeked in.

"Hi, Gavin." Amelia didn't shy away as she usually did. "We were just talking about you."

"Really?" He folded his arms over his chest and leaned on the side of the door. Cocking his head, he looked like a model from one of those pin-up calendars for bachelorette parties or female dorm rooms.

Amelia walked over, and as he stepped aside, she went down the steps, leading Gavin to the tree that was next to her truck.

"You look really pretty today, Amelia." He leaned in close. "Would you like to join me for dinner once you wrap things up here?"

"That's a very nice offer, but…"

"Wait. What's that?" He pointed to the back of the Pink Cupcake. "It looks like you've got a flat tire."

"What?" Amelia whirled around and squinted at the back tire, which appeared to have sunk into the ground. "Oh, you have to be kidding me." She tipped her head back, and her shoulders slumped. "Of all the rotten luck."

Just then, a familiar white van pulled up along the street behind the row of food trucks. It stopped, and the man Amelia had just met the previous day waved and hopped out of the cab.

"Amelia Harley!" He sauntered up to the truck as if he and Amelia were long-time friends, extending his hand to shake. "You know, after you came to see me yesterday, I saw the write-up for your food truck in NUVO. I thought I'd come by and give your cupcakes a sample."

Putting on her best poker face, Amelia smiled and shook Tim's hand enthusiastically.

"Well, Tim, that's really nice of you." Without hesitation, she introduced Gavin and suggested Tim try his Philly cheese steak sandwich. "I've actually got a bit of a situation that I need to make a phone call about."

Amelia pulled out her phone, but before she could dial Dan's number, Tim spoke.

"Is it that flat tire?" Tim's face held a sadistic edge in each crease of his smile. Like looking into a two-way mirror, Amelia saw both the face Tim showed the world and the face he showed David Scranton and Preston Dwight.

She couldn't prove it. Not yet. But she was sure he killed them both. If she had any doubts before, they were gone in the blink of his eye. She was also willing to bet the day's receipts that Tim had something to do with her flat tire.

"Y-Yeah," Amelia stuttered. "Gavin just pointed it out. I don't know what to do. This is a new one for me."

"Well, I've got an Ultimate Fix-A-Flat in my van. I'd be happy to hook that puppy up and get your tire filled." Tim rocked on his heels.

"They've got those for semitrucks, too," Gavin added. Amelia knew he was trying to be helpful, but he really wasn't helping at all. "I've been meaning to get just that thing for my truck. You just never know what you might drive over."

"Yeah, right?" Tim nodded at Gavin. "People just throw rusty nails, glass, anything in the grass. It's well worth the investment. What do you say, Amelia? Are you going to let me help you?"

Shaking off a shiver, Amelia nodded. What else could she do?

"Sure. I appreciate it, Tim. I really owe you one."

"It's settled. Let me just get it from the back of my van." Tim turned and started to walk away, when Gavin spoke.

"What a nice guy." Gavin said it as if it were a secret. "It's a good thing he happened to be passing by."

Amelia looked at Gavin as if he had suddenly turned green.

"I better help." She left Gavin standing under the tree and walked up to the back of the van.

Chapter Twelve

"Can I offer you a hand, Tim?" Amelia asked.

As she leaned around the door, she caught a glimpse of a strange coincidence. Tim was pulling the Fix-A-Flat out of a bag as if it was brand new. Quickly, he stuffed the bag into a corner of the bed, behind some cords and the vacuum cleaner.

"Oh, ah, no, Amelia. I've got it." He whipped around, smiling. "This takes seven minutes. At least it has in my experience." He yanked up the box up by its handle and headed toward the drooping end of the Pink Cupcake. Folding her arms over her chest, Amelia looked into the van.

Pipes. Plungers. A hair dryer? What in the world was a hair dryer used for? Leaning a little closer, Amelia caught a glimpse of the cord. It had a wavy design going through the center of it. The same kind of pattern she saw on the crime scene photos Dan had shown her.

The thought walked through her mind like a tourist strolling along the beach. It didn't jump at her or shock her. It came into focus simply, almost pleasantly, as if saying, "Here you go, Amelia. Now be a dear and pass this information along to Dan. He'll know what to do with it."

As she stood there, feeling a cold draft brush over her shoulders, she also saw an icepick in the toolbox on top of wrenches, screwdrivers, a hammer, and a couple baby jars filled with screws and washers. She stifled a shiver.

Slowly, she walked to the back of her truck, where Gavin was eagerly watching with intense fascination as Tim hooked up the inflator to the tire and began the inflating process. They were chatting about something, but Amelia basically heard all of it like mumbling from another room. Standing back out of the way, she watched in a trance, but then she snapped out of it at Tim's loud voice.

"Uh-oh," he stated. "Looks like you've got a bit more damage than just a flat. Looks like something pierced your tire. See here?" He pointed, and Gavin leaned in like an eager student in shop class. "The stuff that fills the tire is coming out this other end. It's not a big hole, but it probably won't hold you to get to a service station."

"That really makes me mad." Amelia clenched her teeth. "You know, if only I knew who did this. I'd string them out to dry." She stared right at Tim.

"Easy, tiger," Gavin teased her. "It could just be an accident. Like Tim said, who knows what kind of stuff gets tossed on the ground."

Amelia slowly approached the tire, her arms still folded in front of her.

"Looks like someone poked it with something." She stood up straight, switching her weight from her right foot to her left.

It was one thing to try and intimidate her with drive-bys and tails. It was another thing completely to attack her business. Amelia wondered just who Timothy Casey thought he was. Looking intently at his profile, she watched him nod and agree with her.

"Can you think of anyone who might want to do something like this?" Tim said. "Anyone who you may have accidentally offended, intruded on? You know, Amelia, your cupcakes are fantastic. I wouldn't be surprised if one of the other bakery trucks down Food Truck Alley wasn't feeling a pinch since you got here."

Gavin was annoying in his complete unawareness of what was going on. But Amelia stared at Tim and made sure he knew she was staring at him.

"I don't think that's it." Her voice was low and serious. "In fact, I think I better call my boyfriend to come and check this out. Detective Dan Walishovsky. Do you know him, Tim? You said you knew every uniform in the surrounding area."

Amelia pulled her phone from her pocket. As she did so, she saw Tim's jaw clench and unclench, rolling the skin and making it pulse.

"Can't say I do," he said. "I don't think you need to call him."

"What are you talking about? Someone popped my tire. There are surveillance cameras everywhere around here." Amelia pointed to all the buildings on the adjacent streets. She wasn't sure of what she was saying. But it sounded good, and from the look on Tim's face, she was making him madder and madder by the second. "I'll bet somewhere one of them caught something. My gosh, Gavin, your truck could be next. This isn't something we want happening while we're trying to run our businesses. Am I right?"

"Yeah," Tim interrupted her. "The last thing you want is someone trying to ruin your business."

"Maybe you're right," Gavin added, looking clueless.

Tim blinked at Amelia. He nervously wiggled his fingers at his sides like a cowboy at a shootout waiting for the clock to strike twelve so he could draw.

"I'll get Dan over here." Amelia smiled.

"Well, this obviously isn't going to work." Tim leaned down and quickly pulled the inflator tube from the tire. "I'll just get out of the way."

"No, Tim. You should stay here. I know Dan will want to talk to you, and you did try to do a nice thing. He'll be here in no time."

Tim began walking toward his van.

"Sorry, Amelia. I've got something else to do. I forgot I've got an appointment."

"Oh, someone with a backed-up toilet need help? Tell me this, Tim. Do they have any children?" Amelia almost growled the words.

"As a matter of fact, they do." Tim didn't say another word but tossed the Fix-A-Flat kit in the back of his truck and slammed the doors shut. He stomped angrily to the front of the truck, climbed in, revved his engine, and within seconds was out of sight.

"That was weird." Gavin put his hands on his hips. "What a weird dude."

"Yeah." Amelia felt a twist in her gut. Something was wrong besides her flat tire. Looking at the ground where the rubber had spread out in a sickly pool around the hubcap, she chewed her lip. "What am I going to do about this?"

"Well, I might not be quick enough to have the Ultimate Fix-A-Flat in my truck, but I do have Triple A. I'll give them a call, and we'll have you fixed up right in no time."

"That's going to require a tow, isn't it?" Amelia wanted to spit, she was so mad. Tim did this–she knew he did. She showed up where he worked, so he was going to return the gesture in kind and drive the point home that she'd better back off.

"Yes, more than likely."

Lila peeked her head out the door. Apparently, she hadn't been listening to any of the conversation and had been engrossed in finishing the receipts.

"Are you holding on to something?"

"No, Lila. Why?"

"You cleared over eight thousand dollars today. Cleared it." Lila mouthed the words "eight thousand" so no one would hear. When it came to money, Lila trusted no one, which was probably a good idea.

"Great. That ought to pay for the tow and the new tire." Amelia scowled.

After another ten minutes of complaining and fussing over her tire, Amelia flopped down on the back step and affectionately rubbed the side of the truck.

"Well, that must have been why business was so good today. Heaven knew I was going to need the extra cash."

Gavin knelt down on one knee in front of her and took both her hands in his.

"I'm sorry you've had such a bad night. Look, once the tow truck gets here, let me take you to dinner to get your mind off things. Maybe we could have a drink somewhere and talk. What do you say?"

"I can't tonight. In fact, that's what Lila and I were talking about before the whole flat tire took over the afternoon." Amelia gently pulled her hands away from Gavin's. "You are a really nice guy, Gavin, but I'm seeing someone."

Chapter Thirteen

Gavin watched Amelia's face while she explained her situation with Dan, how she felt about him, and how she hoped it wouldn't make things weird working next to her.

"So you were serious when you said you had a boyfriend. I thought you were bluffing. Is he that tall dude who's always wearing a suit that I see over here sometimes?" Gavin asked sheepishly.

"Yeah." Amelia felt her cheeks puff out as she smiled.

"Well, he seems like a decent enough guy. But do you think..."

As Gavin was speaking, Amelia's phone began to ring. She pulled it from her pocket.

"One second, Gavin. It's my kids." She pressed the little green button and put the phone to her ear. "Hey, Adam. What's up?"

"Mom, did you schedule a plumber to come to the house today?"

Amelia froze.

"What?"

"Yeah, there's a guy here who says that you told him to come check the bathroom sink. That you were going to meet him here? You didn't say anything, so I was wondering..."

"Adam, is he in the house?"

Gavin stared at Amelia, whose complexion had gone sheet white. He reached out toward her as if he were scared she might fall over.

"No, he said he was getting a few things from his truck. Meg's at the front door, and..."

"Adam, tell her to shut the door!" Amelia screamed into the phone. "Shut the door! Adam, tell her to shut the door!"

Adam yelled their mother's instructions at Meg.

"Adam? Did she do it? Adam, lock the door! Make sure every door and window to the house is locked! Right now! I'm on my way!"

Gavin stood and tried to put his hand on Amelia's shaking shoulder.

"Amelia, what's the matter?"

"I've got to get home! My kids are alone, and he's there!"

With shaking hands, Amelia dialed Dan's cell.

"Walishovsky."

"Dan! Tim Casey is at my house! The kids are alone there! Please, you've got to send someone to check on them!"

"Amelia, I need you to calm down. Why would Tim Casey be at your house?"

"I don't know. To send a message. To hurt my kids. Dan, I don't have time to explain! Please, send someone to check on them. I won't get there fast enough!"

By this time, Amelia was crying. Lila had come out of the truck when she heard her screaming. She looked at Gavin, who shook his head and was just as confused as she was.

"Oh no!" Amelia hung up the phone and paced toward Lila then to Gavin. "What have I done? I need to get home."

"I'll drive you," Gavin offered. "My car is right over there."

"Yeah, just go, Amelia. I'll handle the truck. Don't worry about a thing."

Amelia looked at Gavin. Wiping tears and mascara down her cheeks, she managed to choke out a thank you as he took her by the hand and led her swiftly to his car.

Within seconds, they were on the road, heading in the direction of Amelia's house. Adrenalin raced through Amelia's body, and without thinking, she explained the whole situation to Gavin. The visit to Waterware, the spontaneous visit to the No-Tell Motel, the backed-up toilet, and the suspicious behavior of Tim Casey in the white van with red lettering, and showing up just as she had a flat tire.

"And now he's at my house. He lied to my children. He saw their faces. Gavin, what if we're too late? My God! What if he's hurt my kids?"

"Don't think that way, Amelia." Gavin tried to soothe her as he sped down the street, weaving between cars and honking his horn. "If everything you think about the guy is true, then he isn't stupid. He won't try anything in broad daylight, and not with evidence stacked so high against him. He's obviously trying to scare you."

"Well, he's done it!" Amelia cried.

After what felt like hours, following Amelia's shaky directions, Gavin finally turned down her street. There was a squad car in front of the house, as well as Dan's car. There in the driveway was the white Waterware van, the back doors open with tools and supplies spilled on the ground.

Officer Darcy Miller was kneeling down at the back of the truck, cradling her arm. Several drops of blood had fallen to the pavement.

Before Gavin could put the car in park, Amelia jumped out and ran up to the officer.

"Oh no. Darcy. Are my kids okay?" She stopped and swayed unsteadily as she reached down to help the wounded officer.

"He caught me with an ice pick. An ice pick! Who does that?" Officer Miller sounded more annoyed than hurt.

"My gosh!" Amelia cried.

"I'm okay, Amelia. Don't worry. Go ahead..." Officer Miller pointed toward the front door.

"Mom!" Meg yelled. She was crying too and came running out into her mother's open arms.

"Where's your brother?" Amelia kissed and hugged her daughter tightly.

"He's in the house with Officer Radcliff. I think that's what his name is."

Taking her daughter by the hand as she'd done when she was little, Amelia quickly hurried into the house. There she saw Adam, visibly shaken, sitting with Officer Radcliff, who had a gentle hand on the boy's shoulder.

"Mom." Adam got up slowly and went to his mother. She took him into her arms, where he buried his head into her shoulder.

"Are you all right?" Amelia kissed his head, still holding Meg's hand.

"Yeah," Adam said into her neck. "Mom. I'm glad you're home."

Amelia looked at the police officer.

"What happened?"

"I didn't mean to open the door, Mom." Meg sobbed. "I looked first, and I thought, 'Oh, he's just a plumber. Maybe he's at the wrong house.' Or maybe you had forgot to tell us about something getting fixed."

"It's okay, Meg," Adam said soothingly. He looked at his mother. "He must have heard me yelling. Before Meg could shut the door, he came barging in. He pushed Meg, and she fell on the floor."

Meg began to sob again, squeezing her mother's hand tightly.

"So I ran at him. I tossed your measuring spoons at him, and when he reached to catch them, I pushed him out the door."

"You tossed my measuring spoons at him?" Amelia laughed and cried while smoothing Adam's hair away from his face.

"I read somewhere that it is nearly impossible for a person to not reach up to grab a set of keys that have been tossed to them. I didn't have keys, so I thought the measuring spoons might be close enough. They were."

Amelia burst into hysterical sobs of relief, and she hugged her children. They just stood there for a few moments, holding each other as Amelia repeated over and over, "I'm so sorry. This is my fault. I'm so sorry."

Finally, they all calmed down.

"You guys sit down. I saw Dan's car out front. Where is he?"

"A squad car showed up right after you called and we got the door shut." Adam wiped his eyes and took a deep breath. "The guy wouldn't listen to the officer when she told him to drop what he was holding."

"Where were you guys?" Amelia rubbed her arms to stop them from trembling.

"We were in the window," Meg replied.

"In the window? Why were you in the window? You should have been upstairs, locked in my room, and on the phone with police."

Meg and Adam looked at each other and smiled through their tears.

"Well, we didn't want to miss anything." Adam sniffled, wiping his nose on his sleeve and grinning.

"Now that it's over, it *was* pretty exciting," Meg added, also wiping her eyes but smiling.

Amelia shook her head.

"So where is Dan now?"

"The guy took off running." Meg sobered up quickly. "He headed through the neighbor's yard."

Amelia looked toward the front door, which was still open. There were two more squad cars and the paramedics out front, their red and blue lights drawing out every neighbor as if they were peculiar moths to gawk and see what was going on.

"You guys stay inside," Amelia ordered them. Heading up the porch was another uniformed officer, who met her at the door.

"Hi, Ms. Harley. We need to talk to Adam and Meg."

"How do you...?"

"Detective Walishovsky has talked about you guys." The officer was short and had a moustache and gentle eyes. "It won't take long. We'll need a statement from you, too. And don't worry about the van. The tow is on the way to pick it up. It's evidence now."

Amelia nodded.

Neither of her children protested. Instead, Meg scooted her chair closer to Adam.

Amelia walked out toward the ambulance. Before she got to it, the two additional squad cars sped off, lights blazing and sirens wailing.

Just then she remembered Gavin. He had parked his car a bit behind the police cars. When he saw Amelia, he climbed out and jogged up to her.

"Are you okay?" He looked genuinely concerned as he slipped his hand around her arm.

"Thank you for driving me."

"It was no problem. Do you want me to stay? I can stay with you for a while if you want." He really looked eager to help.

"No. Please go home, Gavin. I'm going to wait for Dan." She squeezed his hand, patting his fingers and smiling weakly.

Gavin nodded.

"I'll see you at work." He waved as he turned and jogged back to his car. That was going to be a weird environment now. It didn't take dating the guy to cause awkward feelings and bouts of humiliation. Just a lunatic with a hair dryer and an ice pick to do it.

Shaking her head, Amelia went to the ambulance.

"Darcy, have you heard from Dan?" Amelia watched as the EMT bandaged up Darcy's arm where Tim had stabbed her with the ice pick.

"They went to get him." She nodded toward the cars that had just left. "Shots were fired."

Swallowing hard, Amelia looked at the ground then at Darcy.

"We're talking about Detective Dan Walishovsky, Amelia. Don't worry."

"I can't help it." Amelia began to cry.

Chapter Fourteen

After the police had gotten their statements from Adam, Meg, and Amelia, the house and street turned quiet. Adam and Meg had fallen asleep in their mother's bed, not wanting to sleep in such far corners of the house. Not tonight. Not after all the commotion.

Amelia had been in the bed between them as the television quietly buzzed some old western on Meg's favorite classic movie station. Adam gave no protest to leaving the station on. Within ten minutes of all of them climbing into the bed, the kids were asleep. Amelia was anything but.

After inching herself out of the bed, she went downstairs, poured herself a glass of wine, and sat down at the kitchen table. Tears flooded her eyes, and she cried again.

The guilt of the terror she had caused her children to endure was too much, and she shook her head in disgust. Thoughts she'd never dared bring to the forefront of her mind suddenly appeared attractive and possible. Would the kids be safer with their father?

"If he wanted them full time, he would have fought for them, Amelia," she whispered. But she knew once the story hit the papers, John would be blowing up her phone with a laundry list of criticisms. Probably every threat imaginable except that he'd take the kids away. Jennifer wouldn't go for that.

As if on cue, her phone went off. Sweeping it quickly off the table, she let out a gasp as she saw the familiar number.

"Dan. I've been so worried."

"Is my car still in your driveway?" His voice was calm, slow and like music.

"It is." She wiped a tear off her cheek.

"Mind if I come over to get it?"

"Of course not."

"You wouldn't happen to have some coffee, would you?"

"Always."

"Great. I'll be there in a few."

Quickly, Amelia got a pot of hot coffee going and pulled down two cups from the cupboard. She saw the squad car drop Dan off, and when he came up the walk when she opened the door, Amelia thought he had aged ten years.

"Dan?" Her voice cracked.

He shook his head and stepped into the house. Letting out a long sigh, he took Amelia in his arms and hugged her tightly.

"Did he get away?" Amelia's heart was frantically beating against her ribs. "Is he still out there?"

Dan just held Amelia without saying anything.

"He used the cord of a hair dryer to strangle Preston Dwight and David Scranton," Amelia said. "I saw it in the back of his van. Why he had that in the back of his van, I don't know, but the pattern matches the marks in the picture. Perfectly."

"Plumbers often have hair dryers," Dan mumbled into Amelia's shoulder. "If they can't find a leak, they use it to completely dry a spot so they can see the water right away."

"Oh, that makes sense."

Amelia pulled away and put her hand on Dan's cheek. She took his hand and led him to the kitchen.

Even with cups of coffee in front of them, Dan wouldn't let Amelia's hand go.

"When you called and said he was after the kids, I didn't think about who you meant. I just thought I had to get here quickly. It wasn't until I got here and saw it was Tim Casey that I remembered you had said his name."

Amelia's breath caught in her throat.

"I'm so sorry, Dan. It's all my fault." She explained what she had done and how Tim had followed her and had popped her tire but pretended to be in the neighborhood to offer a helping hand. She confessed to putting her children in danger.

"I don't know how I'll ever forgive myself. The kids are going to have to testify, too, aren't they? Or...did he get away?"

He took a sip of coffee. Letting out a deep sigh, Dan looked sadly at Amelia. He shook his head.

"Tim Casey committed suicide when I had him cornered in the garage of one of your neighbors two blocks over."

Amelia gasped.

"He had no intention of going quietly. In fact, he had no intention of going at all. Things were closing in on him."

Dan went on to explain that Starla-Ann Dwight had used him to get her baby's father jealous. It worked. Kyle was back in the house on Preston's last night alive.

"In his warped, twisted mind, it was the boy's fault Starla-Ann wanted to cling to Kyle. Remove the boy, then Kyle would be of no use. Tim could then swoop in. So he had the boy open his bedroom window, and he took the boy out and strangled him in the back of his van with the hair dryer cord. Then he left his body in the park, just tossing it aside like nothing. The problem was that Starla-Ann didn't want anyone after she lost her boy. Tim's plan backfired."

Amelia leaned forward and listened as the coffee in front of her started to go cold.

"Since Kyle already had a bad reputation with the police, Tim assumed they'd take him into custody. But there was no proof Kyle did anything. And Tim was a stellar citizen. Helping with the search party, trying to console the grieving mother. He was the only one with a clean background, so no one ever took him seriously as the murderer."

"But when David Scranton came looking around, that spooked him," Amelia added. "Oh my gosh. He was the plumber for that motel. It's no wonder there was no sign of a forced entry or struggle. Tim probably just knocked on the door and said he was there to fix a pipe or something." She nearly choked. "Like the Boston Strangler." She grabbed Dan's arm. "And he used the same weapon both times. That cord."

"Tim Casey was a popular guy around town."

"I saw his office. Did you see the pictures with all kinds of local celebrities?" Amelia asked. "Aldermen. Cops. Businessmen. I'm surprised he offed himself. A guy like that with all those connections would probably be able to get a fancy lawyer and have a good shot at beating the whole thing."

Dan agreed.

"But he blew it when he came after your kids." Dan cleared his throat. "Something you did drove him into the light. He played a bad hand, Amelia. You had done something to stack the deck against him."

Amelia leaned back in her chair. "No. I didn't do anything but ask a couple questions. None of them were even that good. You'd have been pretty disappointed in my detective skills, Dan. I promise you that."

"But you did the one thing that Starla-Ann didn't do. You pushed. Preston wasn't even your child, but the love you've got for your own kids made you look into this. You were trying to help a mother. Not solve a murder. A man like Tim Casey had no idea what hit him."

Before Amelia could say another word, a groggy Meg came down the stairs, rubbing her eyes.

"Hey, sweetheart," Amelia cooed. "Doing okay?"

"Yeah, I just wanted a drink of water." She stood in a pair of sweat shorts and a baggy T-shirt with a picture of Elvis on it that she had begged for two Christmases ago.

"I'll get that for you." Amelia stood and got a bottle of water from the fridge and cracked the seal open. "Is your brother still sleeping?"

"Uh-huh." Meg took the bottle and two big gulps before kissing her mom on the cheek. "Good night, Mama." She turned to Dan and did the same. "Good night, Dad."

"Good night, honey," Dan replied, his eyes moist with tears of affection.

"What did you say, honey?" Amelia asked softly, knowing exactly what she had heard.

"I just said 'Good night, Dan.'" The muzzy teenager shuffled back to the steps, heading back up to her mother's bed.

Amelia sat down next to Dan again.

"I think the kids would appreciate it if you stayed the night. I know I'd feel better tonight if you did."

Dan slipped his arm around Amelia's waist and pulled her close to him.

"I'd feel better if I did, too."

Chapter Fifteen

It took some time for the tire to be repaired on The Pink Cupcake. Thankfully, after a little research on Lila's part, they found out the flat tire being done through a suspected act of vandalism was not only covered under her insurance policy, but paid out double.

"So that isn't too bad." Lila polished her nails on her shirt, giving Amelia a wink and a bump with her hip as she scooted past her to take up her station at the order window.

"I'm not going to complain. I actually must have needed that week off. I slept in every day. I let the kids stay home one day, but as soon as they found out they were on the news in regard to the suicide of Tim

Casey, they were ready to face the many questions of their peers."

"I don't mean to be morbid, but if the kids can get a little joy out of what that monster did, I say let them. When you're dealt lemons..."

"Speaking of which! Taste these."

Amelia had perfected her newest creation inspired by the words of her boyfriend over lunch and crime scene photos just nine short days ago.

"I call them Lemon Drops," Amelia boasted. "So anyone can have lemon cupcakes, but I dropped in just a pinch of almond and squeezed fresh lemon juice into the frosting. So there is a real zing to it. The candy lemon drops on top were Meg's idea."

"You know who will love these? Teenagers. They love sour candy for some reason." Lila took a bite, getting a tiny dollop of frosting on her nose. Her eyes practically rolled to the back in her head. "It's like a slice of lemonade," she gushed. "Second best after PB and J cupcakes."

"I concur." Amelia helped herself to a bite of the cupcake in Lila's hand.

"Dare I ask what John had to say about it?" Lila quickly took another huge bite.

Amelia took a drink of water from a bottle she had on the table and shrugged.

"He said everything except that he thought the kids were better off with him. He loves the idea of parenting from a distance and being up close Friday night through Sunday morning." She took a napkin and wiped her mouth. "I had to hang up on him a few times."

"Have you ever mentioned it to Dan?"

"No. It's none of John's business that I am seeing Dan, and Dan is too good of a guy for me to get him involved with John's neurosis."

From outside the truck, Gavin yelled his hellos without stopping to chat.

"What did you do to that poor guy?" Lila looked angrily at Amelia. "You may not have found his advances charming, but I was enjoying the view. Now I have to catch it on the fly when he's giving out samples or picking up litter from around his truck."

"I think showing up at my house with enough cops to be in a Macy's parade scared him off."

"I don't know." Lila took another bite. "He still strains his neck to watch you if you are outside. I've seen him do it."

"Whatever." Amelia shook her hips. "Girl can't help it."

Recipe 1: "Lemon Drops" Cupcakes

Makes 12

Ingredients:

- 1 1/2 cups all-purpose flour
- 2/3 cup milk
- 3/4 cup white sugar
- 1/2 cup butter, room temperature
- 2 eggs, room temperature
- 2 teaspoons lemon extract
- 1/2 teaspoon baking powder
- 1/4 teaspoon salt
- 5 drops yellow food coloring (optional)

Frosting:

- 1 cup icing sugar
- 3 tbsp butter, softened
- 2 tsp lemon extract
- 1 tsp milk
- 5 drops yellow food coloring (optional)
- lemon drops

Preheat oven to 350 degrees F. Line muffin tin. Beat white sugar, butter, eggs, and lemon extract until smooth and creamy. In another bowl, sift flour, baking powder, and salt. Add flour mixture to butter mixture, along with milk.

Add food coloring (optional).

Divide batter among muffin cups. Bake for 15-20 minutes, until a toothpick inserted into cupcake comes out clean.

For frosting:

Beat butter, lemon extract, and milk together until smooth. Add food coloring (optional). Beat icing sugar into mixture.

Pipe frosting onto cooled cupcakes. Top with lemon drops.

Spread on cooled cupcakes.

Recipe 2: Chili Cornbread Muffin

Makes 12

Ingredients for Cupcake:

- 1 1/2 cups all-purpose flour
- 1/3 cup cornmeal
- 1/4 cup sugar
- 1/4 cup brown sugar
- 3 tsp baking powder
- 1/4 tsp salt
- 1/2 cup skim milk
- 1/4 cup vegetable oil
- 1 large egg, lightly beaten
- 4 ounces canned green chilies, chopped

Preheat oven to 400 degrees F. Line muffin cups in tin.

Whisk flour, cornmeal, sugars, baking powder, and salt in a bowl.

In another bowl, mix together the rest of the ingredients. Add to dry ingredients, stirring until blended.

Pour batter into muffin cups. Bake for 15-20 minutes, or until top springs back when pushed. Let cool in pan before serving.

About the Author

Harper Lin is the USA TODAY bestselling author of 6 cozy mystery series including *The Patisserie Mysteries* and *The Cape Bay Cafe Mysteries.*

When she's not reading or writing mysteries, she loves going to yoga classes, hiking, and hanging out with her family and friends.

www.HarperLin.com

61852870R00113

Made in the USA
Middletown, DE
16 January 2018